AFRAID of the DARK

Gary Repetto

A Mouse Gate™ Adventure

Mouse Gate Press
1103 Middlecreek
Friendswood, Texas 77546
281-992-3131 281-TEL
www.totalrecallpress.com

ISBN: 978-1-59095-337-2
UPC: 6-43977-63371-2

Library of Congress Control Number: 2016944929

Printed in the United States of America with simultaneous printing in
Australia, Canada, and United Kingdom.

FIRST EDITION
1   2   3   4   5   6   7   8   9   10

As always, to Antoinette and our children, Danette, Christopher and Cheryl and their families.

Author Bio

Gary Repetto is a former Chicago high school all-star baseball and football player who later lettered in football and baseball at the University of New Mexico, playing on three consecutive conference championship football teams. After several years coaching major college football, he was the commissioner of a state wide youth football program with responsibilities that included the interviewing, hiring and overseeing of coaches for a 2000 player organization. After coaching he became a corporate recruiter, recruiting and hiring several thousand engineers and analysts in the defense and mining industries over a long, successful career. His first novel, 'Prairie Fire', was published in 2015. Besides 'Afraid of the Dark' Repetto is working on a third novel set in New Mexico during the Cuban Missile Crisis and a series of short stories, 'Chicago Stories, Catholic and Otherwise'. He lives in Arizona with his wife, Antoinette, and their family.

Visit with Gary at: www.garyrepetto.com

About The Book

Afraid of the Dark is a story about a twelve-year-old boy who is mysteriously transported from the present day back to 1969 while visiting Disneyland, finding himself as a star player in the Chicago Cubs dugout during a game late in that storied season when the 'fabulous' Cubs collapsed in September. Trying to fulfill the wish of his loving grandfather, who has raised him, he single-handedly brings the Cubs back to the brink of making it to the World Series. But much stands in the way and the boy finds out that there are more important matters in life than baseball. Tommy Hartnett is faced with overcoming evil to save the life of his future grandmother, whom he has never met as a child.

Preface

For some reason Tommy felt uneasy, like he had one day in January when the Asian Flu was setting into his body which left him deathly ill for weeks. His grandfather opened the door to the restaurant and when he stepped in with his hand on the Mouseketeer hat, Tommy's world began to unravel. He felt a sudden rush as if he were on a Chicago subway train that was speeding by all of the stops. And then he abruptly found himself back in Chicago, but at what seemed to be Wrigley Field in a dugout with men in baseball uniforms. They were wearing Cub uniforms, white with blue pinstripes and blue stockings. The familiar Cub blue and red emblem was on the shirts and the red 'C' was distinct on the blue caps. They were big men with strong arms and shoulders, but for some reason, they didn't seem as big as Tommy would have otherwise felt. They had grim looks on their faces, some pacing the dugout while others sat with legs stretched out.

"What kept you?" an older man in a uniform barked in a gruff tone. "See Yosh inside and get suited up."

The face of the man was familiar, but Tommy couldn't place it. The day was bright with a slight chill in the air. He glanced out at the ball field and saw the green leafy vines on the outfield wall and realized without question that he was indeed in Wrigley Field. How on earth did he get here from Disneyland, where he was just a few moments ago, he wondered? And in the Cubs dugout of all places? Then he looked out at the first base dugout across the diamond on the other side of the pitcher's mound and saw that it was full of ballplayers wearing what looked like red and white Philadelphia Philly uniforms. This must be a dream!

"Hey kid, Ron Santo," a stocky man with a dark complexion extended his hand.

"Tom Hartnett," he replied and shook hands. Tommy had never used the name Tom. It was too grown up. It was always Tommy. He felt strength in his hand he had never known before and he realized he was at least a couple of inches taller than Santo, looking down at him.

"We've heard a lot of good things about you. We need the help."

"You have?" Tom replied, dumfounded.

"Hey!" the older man yelled. "Get going. They're not going to hold the game up for you."

Chapter 1

Joe Hartnett dearly loved his grandson, Tommy, with the Chicago Cubs being a close second. As he has done so many days of his retirement, he was watching both play baseball at the same time. It was a sultry day in August and Joe was perched on a bench at the top of the stands of a city park near his home in Melrose Park watching Tommy's little league game with his laptop open to the Cub-Cardinal game. For his seventieth birthday he had treated himself to a specialty WiFi antenna that picked up signals from a Starbucks located just a few yards away.

Joe had a straight back with strong arms and shoulders from years as a baggage handler at O'Hare Field. His high forehead, short graying hair and lean physique were evidence of former military.

"Come on, Tommy!" he yelled through cupped hands as the boy stepped into the batter's box. "Hit it out of here."

A marginal player at best, the twelve-year-old Tommy Hartnett in turn loved his grandfather profoundly. His mother had been killed serving in Iraq when he was two and his father is now working lately in Afghanistan, so his grandfather is serving largely as both mother and father to the boy.

The pitcher was tall and beefy for a little leaguer and he threw the ball hard so that it appeared to be the size of a pea rather than a baseball as it whizzed by a batter. "Strike one!" the umpire bellowed jerking his right thumb up dramatically with Tommy's bat was still setting on his shoulder.

"Come on ump!" Joe yelled. "It was above his head."

In a baggy uniform over his thin frame, Tommy was quite certain it was chest high and not over his head, but it went by so fast he really couldn't say for sure. He stepped from the batter's box to rub his hands dry for a better grip on the bat. He looked up at the top of the stands where his grandfather was stationed and nodded. From third base his coach yelled encouragement and flashed a signal which Tommy acknowledged. He was on his own to hit, which he reckoned unfortunately was not in the team's best interest. Tommy moved back into the box and took a couple of practice swings to ready himself for the pitch. The second pitch was down the middle and he swung but missed it by a foot.

"Way to swing, Tommy," Joe yelled and clapped hard.

Tommy gritted his teeth and prepared himself for the third pitch which came in low but he missed that also.

"That's all right, Tommy. You'll get 'em next time," Joe shouted loudly causing a spectator two rows down and to the left to turn back and shake his head. "That's my grandson!" Joe reproved the onlooker, a heavyset man somewhat younger than Joe, who nodded to be polite.

After the game Tommy took the bench seats one step at a time on an angle to meet his grandfather who was still watching the Cub game.

"Look at that Kris Bryant hit!" he stated pointing at the screen. "Best rookie the Cubs have had since Ernie Banks."

"Ernie was pretty good, huh Gramps?" the boy said halfheartedly for he had struck out every time at bat.

"Awe, he was sweet, Tommy boy. Those wrists of his!" Joe formed his hands to mimic holding a bat and snapped his wrists in a swing. "It looked like he was hitting fungos, but in a couple of seconds the ball was out on Waveland Avenue. Just like that!" Joe reminisced a few moments and then said, "And what a fielder. He had the range of two people."

The boy half-smiled and his grandfather noticed Tommy's gloomy mood. He reached over and pushed back the bill on the boy's sweaty baseball hat that better showed his blue eyes. Tommy fingered his straight blonde hair that had fallen from underneath the hat.

"Sit here with me, son, and we'll watch the rest of the Cubs game and talk some baseball strategy. Then we'll get a hamburger and a malted. How does that sound?"

Tommy worked on a smile and sat straddling the bench a row down from Joe so that he could see the screen of the laptop. He was beginning to forget the strikeouts as he especially enjoyed these precious times with his grandfather. "Okay, Gramps." He looked at the game and asked, "How are the Cubs doing?"

"They're tied in the eighth but they've got the go ahead run on base."

"Is that Bryant on first?"

"He is, Tommy. Montero's up with Rizzo on deck. Rizzo's good so they won't want to walk Montero even though he's hot. But they'll still try to get him to go after a wide one."

The Cardinal pitcher did just that, but Montero didn't bite. In short order the count was two balls and no strikes and Joe Hartnett became excited. "They can't pitch around Montero now. They won't want Rizzo coming up with two on base. They'll give Montero a fast ball, and that's his pitch."

The Cardinal pitcher started his windup and set with his

chin turned slightly to first base eyeing Bryant, and then fired a bullet down the middle. Looking for that very pitch, Montero connected with a powerful swing, rocketing the ball high in the right field bleachers.

"Way to go Cubs!" Tommy yelled, prompting several parents and players leaving the park to cheer. Tommy high-fived his grandfather who then logged off and closed his laptop.

"Let's not jinx them, Tommy," he said. "We'll assume they'll win. We'll get that malt and hamburger now." All was well again with Tommy. His strikeouts were a thing of the past and they were on their way to an enjoyable time.

After having a couple of hamburgers at a stand on North Avenue, they stopped by Peterson's Ice Cream Parlor on Chicago Avenue in Oak Park for malted milks. Tommy always enjoyed a double chocolate malt that was so thick that one could black out having to draw so hard on the straw. By then he had completely forgotten his dismal day at the plate and was eager to talk about the Cubs of old with his grandfather. With his baseball cap off, he had to brush hair from his eyes.

"What happened to the Cubs in 1969, Gramps? You said they had maybe the best team ever."

Joe Hartnett pulled the straw from his drink and licked the end as if it was a cone and shook his head looking down at the table. "1969! That was the year for sure. So many great players. Banks, Williams, Kessinger, Santo, Beckert, Hundley. And pitchers! Jenkins, Holtzman, Selma, Regan. I don't know how many were selcted to the Hall of Fame. But a bunch! They were winning everything. How could they miss being in the World Series? I'd a bet anything they'd go to the Series that year. They were ahead by nine games in August, but then the bottom fell out. They lost everything and those darn Mets won everything.

Then the Mets beat Atlanta easily in the National League Championship. The Cubs would have done the same, and been in the Series. It wouldn't have even been a contest. Who could explain that? All those great players suddenly couldn't hit the ball. The pitchers couldn't get anyone out. Joe thought a few moments and then continued, "I was a young man then, in my twenties. I never gave it a second thought that I might not see the Cubs in a World Series. I just wish they did it in '69. Now....I don't know." He smiled and winked at his grandson. "I'm not getting any younger."

"Don't talk like that, Gramps!" Tommy chided anxiously.

"Oh, don't worry, Tommy boy. I'll be around for quite a while. I'll see you to be a grown man." He laughed and added, "Besides, we've got our trip to Disneyland coming up next week."

The boy brightened up. "What's it like there? I can't wait."

"Nothing like you've ever seen. Rides and exhibits. It's as if you're going to another world – a Disney world. You know that Walt Disney, the man that started it all, went to high school here in Chicago."

"Really! Where?"

"He went to McKinley High School. It's no longer in existence."

"Wow. He sure must have had good teachers."

Joe chuckled. "I'm sure he did. So you see how important school is?"

"What should I bring on the trip? I've never been that far."

"I'll make sure you have the right clothes. And I'll bring my old Mouseketeer hat for you to wear."

"What's that?" Tommy asked, making a face with the mention of a mouse.

"We all had them. We wore them when the Mickey Mouse Club was on T.V. Television was just getting started then. The kids from the neighborhood all got around our T.V. with our hats with the mouse ears."

"Mouse ears!" Tommy shrieked, prompting several heads in the parlor to turn.

"Like I said, we all wore them when the program was on. And we all had favorites. Annette Funicello was my favorite. She was so pretty and vivacious!"

"I think I heard about her."

"Yes," Joe rejoined sadly. "She was sick a long time and we lost her not too far back." Then he brightened up. "Well, enough of that! Let's get to-go containers for these malts and get on home. You need a bath and to start getting ready for our trip."

Tommy relished his grandfather's zeal and loved these days with him. And he yearned dearly for Gramps to realize his greatest wish – for the Cubs somehow to be in the World Series. If only the 1969 team had fulfilled their calling, Tommy mused.

CHAPTER 2

Several days later grandfather and grandson were packed and off to the airport. The Southwest Airlines flight from Midway to the John Wayne Airport near Los Angeles took most of the day. Tommy had a window seat that he was glued to a good portion of the trip. His grandfather sat in the middle, with a businessman working on a laptop on the aisle. At 40,000 feet the sky was clear, and Tommy was fascinated as he watched the ground pass below.

Farms were sectioned perfectly like the squares on a checker-board, and the Mississippi appeared vast even from such a height. Then there was a great brown and green stretch of the Great Plains that led into the majestic Rockies. He marveled at the vastness of the massive snowcapped mountain range he had only read about in the books at school and seen on television and the Internet. The mountains must be awfully cold, he thought, to have so much snow in late summer. He shivered thinking about it. Tommy looked at his grandfather sound asleep next to him and wondered how he had felt the first time he saw these wonders below. He had likely flown in what was then called a prop plane. Gramps had spoken of such planes but the boy had never seen one. He thought of his grandfather further and wished profoundly again that the Cubs could have given him a World Series back in 1969, as he sadly spoke of it so often.

In time Tommy also fell asleep and was rather disappointed when a flight attendant announced the plane's final approach for landing and realized, looking back through the window, that they had circled out over the ocean to land from the west. His grandfather, who was still asleep, had told him that the landing might be as such. Tommy had been anxious to see the ocean, but the excitement of seeing Disneyland promptly overtook any regret, and he pulled out Gramps' silly Mouseketeer hat from a bag and set it on his head. It fit perfectly, and his grandfather smiled, rubbing the sleep from his eyes.

"We're here, Tommy boy."

CHAPTER 3

Joe Hartnett went all out for his grandson's trip, staying at the luxurious Disneyland Hotel. Though Tommy was eager to begin exploring Disneyland, Joe wisely suggested that he take a swim and then they have dinner. By dessert Tommy's eyes were at half-mast and he nearly fell asleep with a spoon in his hand. He again sensibly agreed to Gramps' suggestion and went to bed.

Well rested the next morning, Tommy proudly wore his grandfather's black hat with ears and was having a hearty breakfast in the hotel restaurant. Then he remembered something about California and said to his grandfather, "Doesn't Grandma live out here?"

His grandfather crooked his head and answered with amusement, "What brought that on?"

"I don't know. I just thought of it."

Joe smiled. "Yes, she does, Tommy boy. Yes, she does." His grandfather seemed to reminisce and then added, "We actually stayed here in Disneyland right after we got married. At this very hotel." He thought back. "I had just joined the Marines and she was mad as can be at me because the Viet Nam war was on at that time. She was against it and afraid I'd get killed."

Tommy thought a moment of the mother he never knew and how war must be a terrible thing. His thoughts then returned to his grandmother. "How come she left Chicago?"

"Well, she really left me. Or we left each other."

"How come?"

"Oh," he pondered a few moments in thought. "I think maybe she just had too much of the sixties in her." He looked down at the floor and then back to Tommy and thought about the boy and his life so far. "You've missed out a lot on motherly love, haven't you, son?"

"I have you Gramps. That's all I need until dad gets back from Afghanistan."

Joe smiled and winked and then changed the subject, putting on his favorite blue Cub hat. "Are you ready to see Disneyland?"

"I'm ready!" Tommy beamed and they got up from the table.

A short walk from the hotel, they entered the wonderful land of fantasy started so many years ago by the man from Chicago. Tommy's head could have been on a swivel for he seemed to be taking everything in at once. They rode the monorail to begin with to get an overview of the wonderful park. Then they visited Tomorrowland and Frontierland and Main Street. Tommy had never seen anything like this, and he yearned to see more. By mid-afternoon, Joe checked his watch and said, "I'm getting hungry. Why don't we go over to the New Orleans Square and get something to eat? I've always wanted to see New Orleans and I see the Café Orleans has a meal called 'Mickey's Cheesy Macaroni'. Macaroni and Cheese is your favorite. How's that sound?"

"It sounds great, Gramps! Let's go."

New Orleans Square was as Joe had imagined the French Quarter might be. He marveled at the narrow brick streets and the French flavor of the buildings with charming balconies and courtyards. But as they approached the Café Orleans, he failed to notice a strange look on his grandson's face.

For some reason Tommy felt uneasy, like he had on a day in January when the flu was setting into his body that left him deathly ill for weeks. His grandfather opened the door to the restaurant and then when Tommy stepped in with his hand on the Mouseketeer hat, his world began to unravel. He could no longer see Gramps who was only a few steps ahead, and he felt a sudden rush as if he were on a Chicago subway train that was speeding by all of the stops.

Suddenly, he found himself back in Chicago at what looked to be Wrigley Field, in a dugout with men in baseball uniforms. Trying to gain focus, he at first thought this impossible because he is in California, but they were wearing the familiar Cub home uniforms-white with blue pinstripes and blue stockings. The Cub blue and red emblem was on the shirts and the red 'C' was distinct on the blue caps. They were big men with strong arms and shoulders, but for some reason, they didn't seem as huge as Tommy had generally seen adults. These players had grim looks on their faces, some pacing along the dugout while others sat slumped on a long wood bench with legs stretched out.

"What kept you?" an older man standing in a uniform barked in a gruff tone. "See Yosh inside and get suited up."

The face of the man was familiar, but Tommy couldn't place it. The day was bright with a slight chill in the air. He glanced out at the ball field and saw the distinctive green leafy vines on the outfield wall and realized without question that he was in Wrigley Field. How on earth did he get here from Disneyland where he was just a few moments ago, he wondered? And in the Cubs dugout of all places! How often had he dreamed of sitting on the bench in the Cubs dugout! Then he looked out at the first base dugout across the diamond on the other side of the pitcher's mound and saw that it was full of ballplayers wearing what looked like red and white Philadelphia Philly uniforms. This must be a dream!

"Hey kid, Ron Santo," a stocky man with a dark complexion extended his hand, introducing himself.

"Tom Hartnett," he replied and shook hands. Tommy had never used the name Tom. It was too grown up. The name had always been Tommy. In shaking Santo's hand he felt strength he had never known before and realized he was at least a couple of inches taller than this ballplayer, looking down at him.

"We've heard a lot of good things about you. We need the help."

"You have?" Tom replied, dumfounded.

"Hey!" the older man yelled. "Get going. They're not going to hold the game up for you."

Santo winked at the young man and cuffed him supportively on the shoulder. Tom left the dugout through a passageway to climb up iron steps and walk through a cage-like structure over fans that were milling back and forth below purchasing hot dogs and drinks. As he was in street clothes, no one seemed to give him much notice. Tom then opened a door to a surprisingly small clubhouse where a middle-aged oriental man wearing a white fishing hat started to select uniform pieces for Tom without his asking.

"I'm Yosh," he said shaking Tom's hand. "Ninety-nine is your number." He handed the young man a white pinstriped uniform shirt, pants, stockings, a cap, a belt and a roll containing underwear, sliding pads and sweat socks. "You need spikes. What's your size?"

Tom looked down at his feet, surmising that the shoe size he remembered couldn't possibly fit on feet that seemed considerably larger than they had ever been. What was going on? Sheepishly, he replied, "I'm not sure."

The equipment manager looked at him strangely. "You don't know your size?"

Tom shrugged his shoulders, and Yosh shook his head eyeballing Tom's feet. "Maybe eleven." He pulled out a new pair of shiny black shoes with steel spikes from a rack. "Try them on."

Tom took the shoes, sat on a bench and struggled try to slip them on. "A little tight."

"Eleven and a half," Yosh said smiling and provided a second pair that fit perfectly. He shook his head adding to himself, "Don't know his size. That's good."

Stripping down and hanging his clothes in a locker with his name printed in ink on a white strip of tape, Tom donned the Cub uniform, realizing for the first time an astonishing notion that he could soon be playing in the majors. A surge of panic suddenly overtook him. The last time he swung a bat was against a little league pitcher that he didn't come close to hitting. What a fool he would make of himself against a major league pitcher. What in the world is happening! What was he doing here? Was this a dream, he wondered again? If so, he wished he would wake up fast. A sudden urge to throw up struck him and he went over to a toilet in an adjoining room and did so. He then splashed water on his face from a wash basin as Yosh watched silently as if he had seen this before.

Wiping his face dry with a paper towel, the young man figured he had better get out to the field before the old man starts cussing him, so he walked across the concrete locker room floor to the door with his spikes clicking loudly. Now that he was wearing a uniform, several fans below took notice of him as he ambled along the rattling iron cage leading to the dugout. He heard a boy ask another who ninety-nine was. No one seemed to know. Actually, neither did the man wearing ninety-nine.

"It's about time," the old man shouted over a man bellowing out the starting lineups for today's game on a loudspeaker. Tom noticed that this man was reading to the microphone from a scorecard while standing alongside the screen behind home plate. He looked to be even older than the gruff man in the dugout. "Sit down there at the end of the bench," the old man pointed directing Tom to where a smiling middle-aged black player was sitting hunched over tapping his cleats in anticipation on the dugout bottom. He patted his hand on the bench seat next to him, indicating a place for Tom to sit.

"Don't let Leo get to you," he said chuckling. "That's just his way."

Feeling completely out of place, Tom appreciated the man's words and sat next to him. Then everyone stood up for the National Anthem with their caps over their hearts. After it ended with a loud roar from the crowd, the voice from the loudspeaker bellowed out loudly, "Play Ball!" With those words nine of the Cubs stepped up from the dugout and trotted toward their positions. It was then that Tom noticed the number 14 on the back of the man that was seated next to him as he gaited smoothly leaning forward out to first base. He recalled that was the retired number for Ernie Banks, remembering the blue flag with the 14 on a left field poll that Gramps had pointed out. His grandfather had mentioned Mr. Banks dying not too long ago.

Stretching forward, Tom looked for the flag in left field but there was none. That man was Ernie Banks, but he's dead now and had to be an old man when he died. What in God's name has happened, he thought?

Where is his grandfather? What year is this and how did he get here? At that moment he noticed a newspaper on the bench on the other side of where Mr. Banks had been sitting, and he reached over to pick it up. On the front page it said 'Chicago American', a newspaper he had never heard of. With an uneasy sense of trepidation, he looked for the date on the front page. His fear was confirmed, leaving his mouth dry when he saw in black print, **September 17, 1969.** He realized that somehow he was now part of the maligned 1969 Cub team that his grandfather had spoken of so often. He turned to the sports section and saw on the first page an article blasting the Cubs, indicating that they were now four games behind the Mets, and falling.

"You here to play a ballgame or read the paper!" the old man named Leo snapped standing at the other end of the dugout, and Tom quickly shoved the newspaper under the bench.

The Phillies started the game quickly scoring two runs with a home run. Hartnett could hear a collected groan from the crowd as the Philly player connected, sending the ball into the left field bleachers. The old man, whom Tom was quite sure was the manager, shook his head and muttered, "Hall of Fame pitcher my eye." Tom glanced away from Leo to avoid his wrath. Then he recalled how his grandfather had spoken of the demise of the 1969 team, finishing the season eight games behind the Mets. A quick calculation in his head of the amount of days left in the season and the number of games still left to fall behind purported that the Cubs would likely not win this game, or hardly any more in the remaining couple of weeks. Why was he here, he wondered? And how did he get here?

It was in the bottom of the ninth inning that he began to gather an inkling as to why he was here, though not necessarily how this happened. The pitcher, he had heard the public address system refer to as Ferguson Jenkins, had settled down and held the Phillies to the pair of first inning runs, with the Cubs scoring a solo run in the eighth. Jenkins was due up with a runner on second, and Leo looked down the bench and pointed a finger at Tom. "Hartnett, bat for Jenkins."

A knot jabbed in Tom's gut. He was to be found out. Should he just tell Leo that there's been a mistake rather than going to out on the field to make a fool of himself in front of 40,000 fans, in addition to hundreds of thousands watching on television? As if by rote he went to the bat rack and selected a Louisville Slugger with tar on its handle that seemed to be about the right weight. Then he looked down at his shoe and noticed that his laces had become undone and sat back down to tie them. By then the umpire, a burly red faced man with sweat streaming down his cheeks, came over to the dugout.

"Come on Durocher, get a batter up there."

Leo gave a hard stare at Tom who fumbled with the bat and then finally emerged from the dugout in the naked light of day. The afternoon had warmed up some with a steady light breeze from the west. In a daze he strode up to the batter's box and barely heard his name announced by the scorekeeper behind him. After a few practice swings he stepped into the box and dug his cleats into the dirt. He was batting right handed against a left handed pitcher, and as the southpaw readied to wind up, the Philly manager called time and approached the mound. He signaled the bullpen midway between first base and right field with his right arm and took the ball from his pitcher who jogged from the field.

Tom stepped back from the box and rubbed his bat handle with the rosin bag the batboy, a youngster about his age before he had appeared at Wrigley Field a couple of hours back, had fetched for him. He watched the right-handed pitcher warm up, firing balls thirty to forty miles per hour quicker than the little leaguers threw. But the ball didn't appear as tiny as it did in his last game. Even with the loud 'pop' of the ball in the catcher's glove, he saw the ball fine and, without realizing it, he was taking practice left-handed swings. As if it were as natural as breathing, he found himself to be a switch hitter, another inexplicable quirk as he had never swung a bat left-handed as a little leaguer. From the on-deck circle he heard murmurs from the crowd, questioning who ninety-nine was. It was time to bat.

Tom reset his spikes in the box, digging them in for traction, and touched the center of plate with the end of the bat. The perfectly balanced wood felt to be an extension of his arm. Fear disappeared as he watched the ball rise in the pitcher's hand above his shoulder. And then the ball hissed toward his head and Tom plunged to the ground to avoid being beaned. A collective roar of boos came from the crowd that was suddenly behind the unknown pinch hitter. Grasping that Tom was their player and he could win the game, it became alive cheering and banging seat benches.

Tom brushed himself off and stepped back into the box. Readying himself, his fingers caressing the bat, he saw the next pitch leave the pitcher's hand, coming true, waist high over the middle. The swing was swift and powerful and exact. The solid crack of the ball meeting the bat perfectly resonated so that everyone in the ball park knew immediately it was a home run.

The ball was still rising when it crashed into the lower right side of the old scoreboard, some 500 feet from home plate. At first, the crowd was stunned to silence and then it followed with a thunderous roar. In just an instant the outlook of the Cub fans transformed from one of misery to that of euphoria. No one had ever hit a ball with such authority at Wrigley, or anywhere else for that matter. Not Ruth, not Gehrig, not Hack Wilson. The old timers in the stands were promptly comparing what they had just witnessed to the old days. Tremendous home runs they admitted, but nothing like this. The crowd was electrified and this experience was beginning to be conveyed over television, where the thousands of viewers hadn't the pleasure to witness the enormity of the blast in person, though it was apparent the homer was remarkable.

Tom Harnett had never rounded the bases after a home run, but now he instinctively strode leaning forward at a modest clip looking at the ground with his hat back. It gave the newsmen plenty of time to snap hundreds of pictures that would be shown that night and the next day. At home plate his Cub teammates mobbed him, shaking his hand and slapping his back. Like he had been doing this all his life, after crossing the plate he turned back toward the dugout and then tipped his hat at the crowd above the third base dugout. It was bedlam with fans cheering and jumping up and down.

After a quick jaunt across the enclosed cage amid cheers below, Tom entered a locker room appearing much different than the one he had left a couple of hours prior. It was full with players stripping off sweaty shirts, talking and laughing back and forth loudly to be heard over the commotion. Cold beer was now available in an iced tub. A clubhouse assistant was handing open cans out to the players and newsmen who were beginning to emerge from the front door leading to the outside.

Still trying to comprehend what had happened, Tom took an open space on a bench and leaned back against a locker to catch a breath. But he had little time to himself as players kept on patting him on the shoulder and leg as they passed, and then suddenly a WGN camera was facing him with a light shining in his face. A young man with a microphone leaned over so that both were in the camera's range. He looked at a note in his hand that had Tom's name as he couldn't remember it, and then started the interview.

"Tom, was the pitch a fastball or a curve?"

"A fastball," he replied, not recollecting it at all.

"When did you become a switch hitter?"

"As far back as I can remember."

"It says you came up from San Antonio. How many home runs did you hit there?"

Not exactly mindful as to where San Antonio was, Tom replied, "I'm not really sure. I just like to do what I can to help the team win." He took his cap off and brushed back thick blonde wavy hair that was previously shorter and straighter.

A reporter with a pad and pencil sat on the bench to his other side as WGN was wrapping up. He was pudgy and about forty wearing an open-collar white shirt. "I'm Bill Daley with the *Tribune*," he said and they shook hands. "Please forgive my ignorance," he started. "But where have you been? Anyone who hits a ball like that must be known by somebody. I heard you were at San Antonio; but, when I called out there, no one seemed to know much about you."

"Maybe it was just a lucky shot," Tom replied humbly.

Daley shook his head with skepticism. "If it wasn't for the scoreboard, that ball would have gone six hundred feet, maybe more. No one has ever hit a ball like that. I doubt if anyone can!"

Tom smiled as the attendant brought him a beer, but he asked instead for a soda.

"I know," the reporter recanted chuckling. "You just did."

"That's right," Tom said and then added, "I'm just glad we won. Maybe we'll get back on the right track."

"Yeah. The Cubs need that." He watched Tom for several seconds and shook his head again. "How about dinner? There's a great German restaurant not too far from here."

"Another time if you don't mind. I've got to wind down some. I understand I have a room at the Drake. Give me a call there."

"I will." He stood up and shook Tom's hand, who found himself wondering how he was now reasoning and discussing matters confidently on an adult level when just a few hours before he thought and conversed as a child.

Once the reporter had left, Tom quickly showered and changed into his street clothes. In addition to the reporter's offer for dinner, he also begged for rainchecks for dinner offers from several players. For now, he just wanted to walk around the neighborhood, since he probably wouldn't be recognized until the television clips appeared on the night's news. This was the time his grandfather spoke of so dearly, and he wanted to see what Gramps had seen firsthand. But before he left he took a moment to look at himself in a mirror as an adult rather than a twelve-year-old. Tall and strong in the chest with a chiseled tan face, he only recognized his eyes that stared back at him in the locker-room mirror. It was then that he was certain he was the same Tommy Hartnett who had awakened that morning in the Disneyland Hotel some forty-six years from now. He took a deep breath and turned toward the door leading to the dugout. He figured the crowd would be waiting outside the front door. For now, he wanted to avoid it.

CHAPTER 4

Tom walked through the old ballpark as he had done so many times with his grandfather. Above in the grandstand he could hear crews cleaning up the rows and aisles. He recalled Gramps telling how he had spent summers on a cleanup crew. One boy was selected to lift the chair seats in a row while another followed with a broom, pushing trash to the isle. A third would then sweep the amassed trash down the stairs to the concourse where large barrels were loaded up. For this Gramps and the other youth would get a free ticket for the next game. It was one of Gramps' favorite stories, bringing a smile to his face every time he told it.

The exit gate to Waveland Avenue was wide open and Tom walked out of the ballpark with his hands in the pockets of white khaki slacks. His shirt was long-sleeved and checked blue and white and he wore a white Scott cap. He was unsure where the clothes came from, and he wondered what was waiting in his room at the Drake. To the west the sky showed streaks of red as the sun began to disappear from the city. Across the narrow side street, firemen lounged on chairs in front of the old station, taking in the start of autumn.

Tom gathered his bearings, remembering that Gramps had often spoken of the days at Wrigley, especially meeting friends at the neighborhood bars surrounding the ballpark after the games. He recalled two in particular – The Cubby Bear Lounge and Ray's Bleachers. The first was across the Clark and Addison intersection behind home plate and Ray's was at the corner of

Waveland and Sheffield. He decided on Ray's, located just a couple a hundred feet away. As he walked along Waveland he passed young men and women who were likely going from bar to bar. All were talking about the game, but it seemed that none had recognized Tom as the bright star they were all applauding.

Found on the southeast corner of the two side streets, the popular bar was now called Murphy's. Tom had stopped there with Gramps once after a Cubs game. His grandfather spoke disparagingly of the new establishment, preferring the old bar atmosphere. But then he added with a smile, "Maybe it was because I was young and wet behind the ears back then."

The crowd at Ray's was beginning to thin out when Tom Hartnett came through the front door. Much of the young crowd would be heading downtown and to Rush Street, leaving the diehard fans to talk baseball and other sports, as they do so much in these taverns. He took a seat at the bar and ordered a couple of hot dogs and a Coke before looking the place over. There were several tables that were older than those he recalled in Murphy's. Out back was a gravel lot with room for four or five cars. If he remembered correctly, an enclosed extension with tables and a back bar must have replaced the parking lot. On the walls were personally autographed pictures to the owner of the Cubs and Bears, the professional football team that also played in Wrigley Field through 1970.

A perspiring heavyset man with disheveled dark hair from a busy day went to work on Tom's hot dogs from a steamer located at the end of the bar near a takeout window. Snapping open the container that let out a cloud of vapor, he clenched a pair of sizable hot dogs that were promptly prepared with all the trimmings for Tom.

He scooped up two dollars from several bills that Tom had placed on the bar and brought back change. Like everything else Tom had no idea where the money came from. He pushed the change back for a tip and started on the dogs. It was his first time tipping, but it felt natural. Tom was ravished and decided to purchase a third dog for another half dollar.

As Tom was finishing his meal, he noticed a young man nursing a beer at the end of the bar smiling at him. His face was familiar though Tom couldn't place it. Tom nodded back and the man picked up his beer and started over to see him. He was trim, about six foot tall with strong tanned arms under a blue Cubs shirt. His thick brown hair covered his ears and he wore Levis frayed at the knees.

"I know who you are," he said sidling up to Tom on the stool next to him.

"You do?"

"Sure. We have the same name. Hartnett." He extended a hand. "I'm Joe Hartnett." Tom gave his grandfather his hand, realizing with a start who he was once he had heard the voice. Joe leaned over and, sensing that Tom wasn't looking for attention, said in a discreet voice, "You sure can hit. There hasn't been a swing like that since Ted Williams."

"It was only one swing," Tom countered. "And what about Billy Williams?" he added, recalling Gramps expounding on the great left fielder so often.

"Billy Williams. A terrific hitter with a sweet swing. No arguing there. But your swing! My Lord, it came off your bat like it was a nuclear blast. It nearly killed the poor sap changing numbers in the scoreboard. It's going to cost a pretty penny to fix that hole." And then he added with a chuckle, "Knowing old man Wrigley, he'll probably take it out of your salary."

Tom Hartnett snickered and finished off his soda while young Joe Hartnett watched him, feeling no pain from a splendid afternoon enjoying the Cubs and sipping beers. And then he said, "You know you're bringing me hope."

"Why's that?" Tom asked.

"Before I die I want to see the Cubs in a World Series. I don't care if they win or lose, just as long as they play in one. This should be the year. We've got the best team baseball's seen in ten, maybe twenty years, but they've collapsed. Right in front of our eyes. And the Mets are nearly unstoppable. A month ago I'd have bet the ranch that the Cubs would win the division. Yesterday I'd have bet just the opposite. But now you've given me hope."

"Well, I'm glad, Joe." Tom wanted desperately to ask a million questions, but felt he presently couldn't. At the same time he craved to be with his grandfather and suggested, "I just had some hot dogs but could go for a good meal. Do you know of some place we can go? I'd like to buy you dinner."

Joe cocked his head quizzically and said, "You want to go to dinner with me? I'm truly honored."

"It's my pleasure. I'm staying at the Drake. Maybe in that direction?"

"I'm meeting my girlfriend downtown at Mayor's Row. They have good steaks. I've got my car parked nearby. Shall we go?"

"Sounds good. Let's go."

CHAPTER 5

Patty Dwyer's father was a firefighter and her mother scrubbed floors at their parish rectory on the north side of Chicago. If it hadn't been for the Viet Nam war, she would have likely followed the path of most good Irish Catholic school girls. Perhaps going to college for a year or two before getting married and raising a proper Catholic family. But after attending the funerals of two neighborhood boys and a favorite cousin, she became fiercely opposed to the war. Much to her father's dismay, as he at first supported the war, she dressed in a defiant manner wearing a head band with a peace symbol over shoulder length flaxen hair and became a fervent participate in anti-war protests throughout the Chicago area. She had been arrested several times and was once clubbed by the police in Grant Park the year before at the 1968 Democratic National Convention. Having warned his daughter to stay clear of this volatile event, he was nevertheless outraged with the police for beating his daughter. It was then that her father began to change his mind about the war, along with much of the country.

Mayor's Row, a restaurant on Dearborn Street, catered to politicians from nearby City Hall, often in private and closed rooms. It was a quant restaurant with a wonderful piano bar. It was there that Joe and Patty met a year ago and have dated ever since. As it was too early for the piano player to begin in the sparsely filled room, Patty was at the main bar with a brass rail seated on an oak chair back stool nursing a stein of beer.

Wearing jeans and an oversized Cub's baseball shirt with a number 14, she was conversing with the manager, a friend from the neighborhood, when Joe walked in with Tom and went up to Patty and kissed her on the cheek.

"How about that game!" Patty shrieked. Along with Joe she was one of a minority of fans who hadn't been utterly dejected by the collapse of her team.

"You should have been there," Joe said.

"I wish I was," she replied now looking curiously at Tom. "Look who's here," she said coyly to the hero of the day. "Tom Hartnett!"

"Hi Patty. It's nice to meet you."

Patty turned to Joe. "I am impressed, honey. A Chicago Cub! *The* Chicago Cub!"

Joe smiled. "We met at Ray's and he's hungry. So here we are."

"Let's eat at the bar," Patty proposed. "Nicholas barely allows me in here dressed in old jeans. He might draw the line for the restaurant."

"The bar's perfect," Tom said and they took stools with Tom in the middle. He took a long look at Patty and, recalling pictures in Gramp's photo album, saw familiarities in her face. It struck him like a hot blast from a jet engine that she might be his grandmother. This is beyond comprehension. He had decided to tag along with Joe, knowing he was, or would be, his grandfather to find out more about him. But he had had no aspirations of meeting his grandmother. He had naturally thought about her in the past, but never believed he would get to know her. Tom pondered on the possibility that she could be his grandmother and wondered how he might learn for sure if that's the case.

They ordered steaks through the bartender and beers for Joe and Patty and a Coke for Tom, after which Joe excused himself to the men's room.

"So, how did you two meet up?" Patty smiled with a cocked head slipping strands of loose hair under her head band.

"I stopped by Ray's Bleachers for hot dogs and we met at the bar."

"But you and Joe seem like you've known each other for years. He makes friends easily, but this is a little surprising."

Tom chuckled, "That happens sometimes."

Patty took a package of cigarettes from a large canvas purse with red peace symbols sewn on and offered one to Tom who declined. She lit one and exhaled away from Tom.

"How serious are you and Joe?" Tom asked starting a conversation in that direction.

"That's an unexpected question since we just met," she replied in a good natured tone. "But since you asked," she continued. "I love him dearly, and he loves me."

A twinge of anticipation ran through Tom's veins perhaps this was indeed his grandmother! Then Patty inhaled strongly and blew smoke down toward the floor. "But it'll never work."

"How come?" Tom probed with disappointment.

She shook her head sadly. "I'm not good for him."

"Why not?" Tom asked.

"Oh, I would just say he's too good for me. Joe will be a splendid father. But he wants kids and I don't." She smiled at Tom, reading his thoughts, and said, "Don't get me wrong. I love kids. I just don't want to bring any into this crazy world."

"Things change," Tom said, concerned that Patty might not

be his true grandmother after all. "They always do. Every parent seems to be faced with uncertainty in bringing up kids," he added, unsure of where this adult insight had come from.

She shook her head and chuckled, "You sound like Joe. He sees the bright side of things, while it's pretty dim for me."

At that moment Joe returned from the restroom, followed shortly thereafter by a waitress bringing their meals from the kitchen. They enjoyed the steaks and Joe and Patty had a couple more beers with Tom polishing off another Coke. When the bill arrived Joe and Tom argued over how to handle it.

"I invited you," Tom maintained. Joe countered, "You're new to Chicago. It's our treat. We always do that."

While they were discussing payment of the check a dapper man in a black suit with a dark complexion that had been part of a threesome at the end of the bar approached them. He looked to be in his early thirties with a strong olive face and wavy slicked down black hair. "We saw you play today," he said to Tom. "My friends and I want to buy your dinners," he said pointing a hand toward to other two men.

Not sure why, Tom shook his head and declined. "That's nice of you but I'm taking care of the bill. We decided that on the way over."

The man's eyes, dark as his hair, studied Tom for a few moments and then he said in a quiet but firm voice, "I insist. Please don't disappoint us."

Joe became uncomfortable, especially when Patty jumped into the exchange. "You offered and we said no. Can't you understand that?"

The man stared at Patty with an empty expression, and then said, "No problem, miss. We just wanted to show our appreciation."

She was about to add something when Joe squeezed her hand as a warning. "Thank you again," Joe said and the man went back to the end of the bar. Tom took care of the bill and they left.

Outside, Patty, still fuming, chided Joe, "You should have punched that smart-alecky jerk in the nose! I don't like him!"

The fall night air was cool with a light mist as cars sped by on Dearborn. Joe snorted, "That wouldn't have been a good idea, my dear."

"Why not? He didn't look so tough."

To Tom he explained, "Patty unfortunately is a little slow recognizing when someone's with the mob. It definitely wouldn't have been a good idea to punch one of them in the nose."

Pouting, Patty said, "I don't care if they're gangsters. I didn't like that pretentious jerk."

Tom didn't say anything, but briefly wondered why a mobster had shown interest in him. He shrugged his shoulders with the thought and said, "I'm going to need some sleep for the game tomorrow. Could one of you drop me off at the Drake?"

"We'll both take you," Joe replied. "Patty took the subway here."

"Give me a number where I can reach you," Tom said. "I'll probably be meeting with a guy from the *Tribune*, but I'd like to get together with you again."

"Wow!" Patty exclaimed, forgetting about the man in the bar. "Mr. Cub wanting to meet with us again."

Joe took her hand and said, "Remember, Patty, that Mr. Cub

is Ernie Banks. It's blasphemy to say otherwise."

She reached up and kissed Joe on the mouth and said, "You're right. Forgive me."

Tom chuckled politely, but deep down felt a tenderness as he was figuring more and more that this was his grandmother.

CHAPTER 6

The next afternoon Wrigley Field was nearly full for batting practice. It was a cool fall day, one that reminded Chicagoans that winter wasn't far ahead. Normally, most fans would spend as much time leading up to a game as possible in the bars surrounding the ballpark. But Tom had become a sensation. Once word spread and films of his home run the day before had reached the news channels, several thousand had sacrificed a few beers to see what the young sensation might do in batting practice.

They were not disappointed. First, he batted left-handed against a right-handed pitcher who threw balls with modest velocity that Tom rocketed into the right field bleachers and beyond. With his pride at stake the pitcher picked up the speed of his pitches, and Tom pounded the ball that much harder and farther. Windows of the homes across Sheffield Avenue were in danger, and residents could be seen opening them with gloves in hand to protect their property as much as possible. The echoing report of the balls smashing off of the fat of the Louisville Slugger caused a continuous buzz throughout the stands.

Then a left-handed pitcher took over, and Tom crossed the plate to swing right-handed. Results were the same, and even more so. Line drives either careened dangerously off the benches in the leftfield bleachers or easily cleared the cat-walk to land hard on the far side of Waveland Avenue. Outside the park kids with gloves had a field day catching or chasing down the monstrous blasts that bounced down the side street north from Waveland. One pitch he pulled hard to the left, passing foul over the wall, causing the men sitting on folding chairs at the firehouse across the street to frantically scatter as the ball banged loudly against the hood of a shiny red hook-and-ladder.

"Hey kid, come over here," Leo Durocher yelled from his spot on the side of the batting cage. Tom dutifully stepped away from the plate and stood by the manager with the bat resting on his right shoulder. Next to him Leo was a head shorter.

"Old man Wrigley's gonna yell at me for losing so many balls."

"I'm sorry, Coach. It just feels so good hitting up there."

"Call me, Leo. Nobody in baseball calls us coach." He spit brown tobacco juice on the ground and lifted his prominent chin to consider Tom a few moments. And then he asked, "You any relation to Gabby Hartnett?"

Tom shifted the bat to his other shoulder and replied, "I don't think so. Who is Gabby Hartnett?"

Leo grumbled to himself and shot another stream of juice to the ground. "He was the Cubs catcher on its last World Series team."

"Sorry. I don't remember him."

Leo took his hat off and brushed back what brown hair he had left and said, "Where did you come from? How come I've never heard of you until the other day?"

"I've moved around a lot," Tom answered, not sure what else to say. "I just never played much organized baseball, I guess."

"Are you kidding? No organized ball and you hit like that!"

Tom just shrugged, which seemed to annoy the

cantankerous Cub manager. He shook his head and said, "I don't know. I want you on the bench until I can figure this out."

"You're the boss," Tom replied fingering the bill on his blue hat.

"You're darn right I'm the boss," he said and walked away.

At game time an hour later when the starting lineups were announced by Pat Pieper, the name of the old man by the screen, a loud collective buzz came over the ball park when Tom Hartnett was not included on the scorecard for the final game of the Phillies series. It was followed by boos when the first Cub up struck out. The intensity of jeers increased as other Cubs followed suit, unable to safely hit against the Phillies' pitcher. Banks struck out, Santo grounded out , Williams and Kessinger flied out, Beckert and Hundley both struck out. All great players who had been extoled by Tom's grandfather so often. By the top of the sixth inning the crowd was furious with the Cubs down by three runs and Tom slouched back on the bench with his legs crossed at the ankles. He kept his hands in a blue Cub jacket to keep them warm.

Leo had been pacing the dugout, cussing to himself. It was as if he had a personal battle going on inside and he had lost. "Get out in center, Hartnett," he bellowed and spit tobacco juice on the dugout floor. He then stepped up and out on the field and announced the change to the home plate umpire. When ninety-nine appeared out of the dugout and began to trot toward center field, the roar from the crowd was thunderous. And then it was repeated as Pat Pieper stated the change through the public address system.

For the first batter nothing remarkable occurred. A lazy foul popup was caught by Hundley behind the plate near the wall.

And then Don Money tripled down the first base line, quieting the fans considerably. It seemed as if the old sorry Cubs were returning and a few fans began to leave. The next Phillie batter worked the count to ball three with no strikes. Those still paying close attention to the game, as true fans did, were suggesting to one another that they should now intentionally walk the batter to set up a possible double-play with a man on first. But a fast ball was thrown, straight down the middle, of all places, and the ball was hammered on a high arc toward left center field. At first it looked to be a home run and the runner on third started trotting lazily home, but held up about just a few feet from the bag just in case. As Tom pushed his back against the vines to be ready for the ball in the event it didn't drop in for a home run, the runner moved back to the bag to tag up, figuring he would have an easy run home. But Money had never seen Tom Hartnett's arm; nor had anyone else in major league baseball for that matter. Nearly four hundred feet from home plate Tom caught the ball high on the wall, and in a single motion, fired it toward home on a line not ten feet off the ground. A collective gasp came from the crowd as the ball reached Hundley's glove three steps ahead on Money, who only had to cover ninety feet.

The Phillie runner was dumbfounded upon seeing the ball waiting for him in the mitt of the Cub catcher a good two or three seconds before he could reach the plate. He was so surprised that he at first desperately thought to accuse the Cubs of engaging a second ball. The ear shattering racket from the crowd lasted well after the Cubs had cleared the field into the dugout. Never had such an arm been seen in baseball, even by the old timers that had witnessed the greats of the teens and 20's such as Ruth, Cobb, Speaker and the Big Train – Walter

Johnson.

Fans chattered non-stop about the throw while waiting fervently for Tom to bat. But it would be two more innings before his turn in the order, and then the bases were loaded with the Cubs still down by three runs. The excitement grew as he stepped to the plate batting right-handed against a strong left-handed pitcher. The first pitch was high, a ball, and a roar of approval came from the crowd. The next two pitches were balls also, neither close to the plate at all. The fans, hungry for a home run, booed the Phillie pitcher furiously. The throng had come to see this new marvel blast the ball out of the park, but it appeared that the Phillies might concede one run and walk Tom rather than allowing four runs on a homer to take the lead. The next pitch was low on the inside corner and the umpire jerked his thumb up for a strike. A loud wave of boos ensued, refuting the earlier taunts for not throwing strikes. Then before the pitcher could begin his windup a Philadelphia coach called time while jogging out to the mound. The hostile throng became even rowdier, targeting both the Phillies and the home plate umpire. It seemed as if the coach and the pitcher were in disagreement about something, and finally the umpire walked halfway to the mound to break them up.

Once play was restored the noise from the banging of seats and forty thousand voices screaming was ear-shattering. The pitcher, with a terrific fastball, wound up slowly and fired the ball down the middle at a hundred miles per hour. He put an extra effort in the pitch which would get past most any batters, but Tom was not just any batter. His swing was swift and natural and most powerful. The ball was met timely and solid and it soared from the heart of his bat toward left field. Still rising as it cleared the wall and then the fence overlooking Waveland Avenue, the ball went clean through an attic window of an apartment building across the street. Kids below with their gloves ready needed to move quickly to avoid the falling glass. The colossal hit brought an eerie hush to the crowd as they collective stood in disbelief. Then a deafening roar erupted.

Putting the Cubs ahead by a run, Tom humbly jogged around the bases and tipped his hat at the rejoicing crowd that had had little to cheer about the past month. All three runners were at home plate to shake his hand, in addition to the rest of the Cub team waiting near the dugout. Santo, Banks, Williams, Holtzman, Jenkins. All of the greats were slapping him on the back and shaking his hand. An announcer, who later stated the ball might have traveled six hundred feet had it not been for the building.

Only Leo was noticeably absent from the jovial reception, and remained sitting at the end of the bench eyeing Tom with a good deal of curiosity. Of all present only Leo had played with and been around the earlier greats – Cobb, Ruth, Gehrig, DiMaggio, Robinson, Ted Williams, Mantle, the banned Shoeless Joe Jackson. They were the best, but none could hit or throw as Tom Hartnett had just done. Not even close. Something was very odd. This was surreal and Leo didn't understand it. This was not the baseball game he knew and grew up with in the early part of the century.

In the ninth the Phillies went three up and three down, giving the Cubs the win. The Mets lost that afternoon, putting the Cubs three games from first place with all the momentum in the world. There was joy and a return of confidence throughout the city. This would be the year after all! The Amazing Mets didn't have anyone who could match Tom Hartnett. But Leo didn't share in the city's excitement for he felt something was just not right. He sent word for Tom to meet him in his office after the game.

Tom showered quickly for he wanted to see Joe and Patty later that evening and hoped the meeting with Leo wouldn't take long. He entered the manager's office running his fingers through his wavy hair so that it would dry in place. With Leo he saw Bill Daley, the *Tribune* reporter, sitting beside the manager's desk. Leo was still in uniform, but had taken off his shirt with only a blue-sleeved baseball undershirt on, wet with perspiration. His stocking feet were up on the desk.

"You know Bill Daley from the *Tribune*, kid," Leo said pointing at the reporter.

"Sure," Tom said and shook his hand.

"I tried to reach you at the Drake this morning," Daley said.

"Sorry. I didn't get the message."

"That's okay. I just had a couple of questions."

Leo broke in, "We're really glad about your play, but some things just don't add up. Why don't you have a seat." He indicated a cushioned metal chair in front of the desk.

"How can I help you?" Tom asked from the chair.

The reporter pushed his straw Fedora back and scratched his head on the side. "I've asked for more information out in San Antonio, and it seems like nobody knows much about you. Your name's on the roster and everything, but I still can't find anyone who remembers you."

Leo dropped his feet from the desk and sat up. "How can anyone hit and throw the way you do and no one take notice of it?" Leo challenged. "Something's haywire here."

Tom leaned back in his chair. He was dressed in tan slacks and a light cashmere sweater with brown loafers; all that had mysteriously appeared in his luggage at the hotel. After a few moments of thought, he answered, "I guess I just didn't get a chance to play much." And then he added, "It's hard breaking in. I just needed a chance."

Leo looked at the reporter and, baffled, Daley shook his head. "Were you in any other organizations? Perhaps even by a different name? A nickname? I pay close attention to the various minor league organizations."

Tom was getting anxious as he wanted to visit more with his future grandfather and probable grandmother. He needed the name of a team to hopefully put off the pair's questions. "The Colorado Rockies," he blurted, throwing out the first team that came to mind.

Puzzled, the reporter and Leo looked at each other. "You mean the Denver Bears?" Daley said.

Remembering that Gramps had mentioned a number of expansion teams had come into being over the years and he realized that Colorado was likely one of those based on their expressions. "Yeah, the Bears," he said. "I always think of the Rocky Mountains when I think of Colorado." And then he added, "I didn't play much with them either. This is actually my first real test as a ball player."

Leo grunted and turned to Daley who shook his head. After jotting a couple of quick notes, the reporter said, "I just don't get it. The team's winning because of you, but what can I write about? Some phantom appears out of nowhere without any known experience and makes major league ball players look like a bunch of high schoolers."

Recognizing how close Bill Daley was to the truth, Tom just shrugged. "I don't know what to say. I'm just trying the best I can."

Leo studied the young man a few moments and then said, "I might as well be talking to the wind. Go on, get out of here."

Tom gladly pushed up from the chair and left the office to meet Joe and Patty, having made arrangements that morning to get together after the game.

CHAPTER 7

The Ivanhoe Restaurant, built in 1920 during Prohibition, served as a speakeasy for the first thirteen years of existence. It resembled a limestone brick castle with an attached theatre-in-the-round and enchanting catacombs below the ground surface. After signing countless autographs, Tom was able to break away from the fans outside the ball park, and took a cab to meet his friends at the famous restaurant.

Looking at the quaint building located on the city's north side at Clark and Wellington Streets, Tom was struck by the beauty of the castle's stone glittering under the bright street lights. He paid the cabbie, adding a generous tip, and took the winding stone stairway down to the catacombs where he was to meet the pair. Unsure of how long this inexplicable journey to the past would last, Tom wanted to spend as much time as possible with these two. The vivacious and slightly inebriated Patty Dwyer was at a piano bar holding a mug of beer singing along to the music provided a heavyset man pounding merrily at the keys of the piano.

"Oh you beautiful doll, you great big beautiful doll..." she belted out gaily to the music, pointing at herself and laughing.

Tom came over and she kissed him on the cheek. He saw that her eyes were glassy and that she had likely had more than one of the beers.

"Where's Joe?" he asked.

"He said he had to stop to do something and will be here in a few minutes." And then she pointed to the piano player. "This is Two-Ton Baker," she yelled over the noise of the room, and the piano player waved with a hand and started to pound out another song.

"Five foot two, eyes of blue," Patty sang out pointing a thumb to her chest. "That's me," she cried and took a drink from her beer. She kissed Tom a second time on a cheek. "You did it again. You won the game."

"It was a lucky hit," he replied in a modest manner.

"No way! You knocked the socks out of it!"

At that moment an elegantly-dressed elderly woman stopped by the piano bar with a Cub's scorecard in her hand and said to Tom, "I took my grandson to the game and he's upstairs in the restaurant. I didn't want to bring him into the bar, but I was wondering if you could sign this for him?"

Tom took the scorecard and smiled, "Sure." She supplied him with a pen.

"What's his name?"

"It's Tommy. Just like you."

Tom wrote, 'To Tommy. Best of Luck' and signed it, 'Your friend, Tom Hartnett.'

The lady glanced down at the scorecard and tears came to her eyes on reading what Tom had written. "Thank you," she said placing a grateful hand on his arm.

"Look at you!" Patty said. "You made their day; maybe their life."

Tom smiled studying Patty for a few moments, and then leaned closer to be heard over the clamor of the bar and said, "I see that you care a great deal for Joe and I think he wants to marry you. He's a good man."

She looked at Tom and then shook her head. "You sure

know how to throw water on a good time."

"I'm sorry, but I see two wonderful people that seem to be meant for each other, and I feel I should say something."

"Listen, I love Tom a great deal. I said that before and I mean it. But marrying Tom means babies, and you know how I feel about that right now."

"Sure," Tom replied. "But you'd be surprised how matters can change for the good."

"In this crazy world? Do you see the news every night? I can't watch it! Boys, younger than us, coming back in coffins all lined up on the tarmac at O'Hare. And maybe they're the lucky ones, not having to live without arms and legs!"

Tom looked at floor and nodded. "I understand, Patty," he said quietly, wishing for a different response. As he was dwelling on her comments, Joe appeared at the bar and gave a Patty a kiss. Though now in a dour mood, she smiled and kissed him back.

Tom relished their intimate touches as he saw their love for each other, but wondered how and when, assuming Patty was his grandmother, that they eventually would get together.

"Let's go to a table," Joe said gently pulling Patty toward a nearby tall table for four. Tom noticed that he seemed to be somewhat nervous and had a strange sense that his grandfather was about to make a momentous announcement that would affect all of their lives somehow.

"What's the mystery, Hartnett?" Patty coyly asked.

"I need a beer first," Joe said and went to the bar to order beers for the three and Patty glanced at Tom with a puzzled look on her face. She tucked a few loose strands of her hair under her anti-war head band as Joe brought the mugs, holding them together with his hands through the glass handles. He set the beers on the table and took a drink from his. It was a long drink that emptied half of the mug. He set it down and cleared his throat. "I joined the Marines today."

"No! No!" Patty screamed causing heads to turn, even over the bar noise. "You can't!"

"I have, honey."

Patty picked up an ash tray and hurled it at Joe, bouncing it off his chest. "You can't do that to me! Or yourself!"

Joe took her hand, but Patty yanked it free while Tom stood back. "Don't touch me!" she cried "I hate you!" And then she ran from the catacombs, disappearing up the stairway.

Joe looked to Tom who shrugged helplessly. There was no way for Patty or Tom, of course, to know that he would survive Viet Nam unharmed to any extent. Tom resolved that he wouldn't be believed anyhow, so he said nothing, watching the painful heartbreak in Joe's face. Feeling badly about Patty's reaction to Joe's enlistment, Tom agreed to join him for a beer at the bar to discuss his situation, but he needed to use the restroom first.

Thinking of what he might say to Joe, Tom found the men's room empty but noticed a familiar face follow him in. It was the unpleasant thug from Mayor's Row, the downtown restaurant at which he first met Patty. At the door behind them stood a large man with a broad chest and a thick neck. He positioned himself to block any others from entering the room.

"Hello, slugger," the first said. In the bright light of the men's room, Tom saw black eyes that appeared not to have pupils. He was wearing a sport jacket with an open collar white shirt and alligator shoes. Tom figured correctly that the meeting was certainly no coincidence and nodded guardedly in return.

"You did it again," the man said with a smile that sent a chill down Tom's back. "You're quite a hero."

"Not so much," Tom replied uneasily.

"Oh yeah. You are a hero, all right. All the fans are getting their hopes back because of you."

"I just play ball the best I can," Tom countered.

The man studied Tom several moments and then said, "My name's Johnny Rome. You might have heard of me."

"I can't say that I have," Tom replied honestly.

"Well, now you have, and you're making me very unhappy."

"Why? I don't even know you."

A callous smile came to Johnny Rome's face. "Let's just say I have a lot to lose if the Cubs go to the World Series. A lot. And I don't want to lose that."

Tom said nothing at first looking down at Johnny Rome, remembering that Joe had identified him as part of the mob. And then he said, "What are you asking for?"

Rome cocked his head and shrugged casually. "You seem to be able to do anything you want with the bat. Just hit fly outs instead of home runs. Lose the ball in the sun. Throw the ball over heads with that arm of yours."

"The Cubs have a lot of talent. They can win without me."

The mobster chuckled. "They're losers. They choke. You're the difference."

"What will happen if I don't do what you want?"

Rome paused a few moments and then sighed as if it was something he didn't want to say. "You seem like a smart guy. I think you know what will happen. And there's that loudmouthed girlfriend. She might not want her face full of acid."

Tom had an urge to put his fist through the smirk on Rome's face, but saw the vicious-looking man at the door take a step in his direction as if he were reading Tom's thought.

Johnny Rome stepped aside and opened his hand indicating the door with an outstretched arm. "Enjoy the rest of the night, and remember what I said."

The one at the door opened it for Tom to leave and he did, wondering how he had found himself in such a fix. Somehow he had been sent back to get the Cubs into the World Series for his grandfather, but he couldn't bring harm to Gramps or Patty, whether or not she would indeed be his grandmother.

CHAPTER 8

Weary from a day of baseball and the incident at the Ivanhoe, Tom shook Joe's hand as he dropped him off in front of the Drake. He hadn't paid much attention to Joe's rambling about how his joining the Marines affected Patty. Tom's mind was on the threats from Johnny Rome, but he did lend encouragement that it all will work out, again not willing to say how. Nodding to the doorman as the man opened an ornate gold door for the ballplayer, Tom didn't at first notice Bill Daley waiting for him on a couch in the vast plush hotel lobby. Wearing a beige trench coat buckled at the waist, the reporter got up and walked toward Tom.

"Out late," Daley said extending his hand, holding the straw fedora in his other one.

"You are, too, I see," Tom replied shaking his hand. "What's up?"

"I did some thinking and there's something that bothers me. Can we sit for a few minutes? I promise it won't take long."

"I do have a ball game tomorrow and I'm pretty tired."

"I promise it won't take long, and I feel it's important to talk about."

"Okay, a couple of minutes."

They went back to the couch on which the reporter had been waiting and sat about a yard apart. They turned to half face each other.

"Can I get you a drink or maybe coffee?" Daley offered and Tom shook his head.

The reporter fingered his hat, moving it nervously around in his hands while he gathered his thoughts. And then he said, "After the game when we talked about your coming out of nowhere, you didn't have much to say." Tom nodded and Daley continued, "I thought on that a while and remembered something that happened last year that I couldn't explain. Still can't for that matter."

"What's that, Bill?"

"I was out in Los Angeles watching the Dodger-Pirates game. I had taken some time off to help my daughter at UCLA. It was in June, June 4th to be exact. I can't even remember who won the game. What I remember is a man named Ted Williams, same name as the great ballplayer, but certainly not him. I was leaving Dodger Stadium when he came up to me, real jumpy like. I could tell he was upset about something." The reporter rubbed his fingers across his chin, with his eyes unfocused above Tom as he thought back. "He was somewhat incoherent, yelling about the need to get to the Ambassador Hotel. It was late in the evening and I was supposed to meet my daughter for coffee and dessert, so I tried to get around him but he latched on to me. Then I asked him why. All I heard then was the name Kennedy."

"Kennedy?"

"Right. I found out later he was talking about Robert Kennedy."

The name Robert Kennedy sounded familiar to Tom, but he wasn't sure where he had heard about it. Perhaps in one of his classes.

"The man actually took ahold of my wrist, begging me to drive him to the Ambassador. I told him I couldn't, but he was persistent. I took him for a kook, but there was something about his manner that made me think otherwise, so I let him walk with me out to the parking lot. Or, rather I walked with him since he was moving at a near run." Daley paused and then continued, "I still hadn't agreed to take him anywhere, but as we neared my car he started crying out that he needed to get there to save Kennedy's life; someone was going to shoot him. I told him he should call the police, but he yelled that there wasn't enough time, and they probably wouldn't believe him anyhow. He had to be there to stop the gunman."

The reporter paused and Tom broke in, "So you drove him to this hotel?"

Daly looked at Tom with a brief moment of puzzlement at the words 'this hotel' as it was well known that Kennedy was killed the year before at the Ambassador and it seemed Tom wasn't familiar with it. But he shrugged it off and continued, "Yes, I drove him. All the way he kept looking at his watch, muttering stuff about how things will be different if Bobby becomes president. It was really weird I tell you. I was starting to feel he might be serious, being that Bobby's brother had been shot just a few years before."

Tom now recalled some of his history. President John F. Kennedy was assassinated in 1963 and he had a brother, Bobby Kennedy, who was also assassinated while running for president. He couldn't remember the year, but it must have been 1968, as Daley said last year and this is 1969. He was assuming that Bobby Kennedy was killed that night, and listened further.

"We might have gotten to the Ambassador in time if there hadn't been an accident on the 110. We were about three blocks away when this Ted Williams looked at his watch and let out a cry and started to sob uncontrollably. I remember looking at the time on the dashboard. It was 11:30." Daley glanced at his watch to simulate as he had with the clock that night. "It was precisely the moment that Kennedy was shot. How could he know that?"

Tom shook his head, pretending dismay. "What happened to him?"

The reporter was slow to answer, continuing to think about that night. "By the time we got to the hotel, police cars and ambulances were everywhere. He got out of the car, and I never saw him again."

Tom nodded and then said, "That is a very strange story, but how come you're telling me this?"

Daley stared at Tom for several moments and then he shook his head slowly and said, "By nature I'm someone that looks for explanations. How can you explain my experience in Los Angeles, and how can you explain your coming out of nowhere-playing ball the way you do?"

Looking down at the floor with his hands interlocked between his spread apart legs, Tom shrugged his shoulders and said, "I don't know, Bill. It does sound strange, especially the guy in L.A., but all I know is I've been brought in to play baseball, and I'm doing what I was asked to do."

The reporter stared at Tom for a few moments and then shook his head in dismay. "Leo's right. I might as well be talking to the wind." But then he stood up and extended his hand and said, "I don't care where you came from. Just keep it up." They shook hands and the reporter left.

Tom thought on what Daley had just said, realizing that

keeping it up now is a very complicated problem. He waved at a couple of well-wishers and went to the elevators to go up to his room.

CHAPTER 9

The next morning before taking a cab to Wrigley Field for the first of the Cardinal three game series, Tom gave Joe a call. He found him in the middle of wrapping up affairs before traveling out to California for basic training.

"I want you and Patty to do me a favor," Tom requested.

"Sure, name it," Joe said sounding surprised. "I can't explain why over the phone, but I need the two of you to leave town immediately."

"Are you serious?" Joe replied with a chuckle.

"I am. Very serious."

"You do sound serious." Joe continued, "What's going on?" And then he added in an uneasy tone, "Why, Patty?"

"You're both in danger. As I mentioned, I can't really talk about it right now."

"Patty's in danger?"

"Yes. I believe so."

"We were planning to be at the game today."

"Where is Patty?"

"I don't know. I can't reach her by phone. She's so darn mad at me, she's probably not answering out of spite."

"We've got to find her, before someone else does."

"You're getting me worried, Tom."

Tom looked at his watch, a Mickey Mouse brand he wasn't sure exactly how he had obtained, and said, "I have a few hours before I have to be at the ballpark. Could you pick me up at the Drake to see if we can find her?"

"Sure. I'll meet you out front on Walton Place in twenty minutes."

Joe pulled up to the Drake in fifteen minutes and Tom was there wearing a windbreaker to cut the chill of the morning.

"Where do you think she might be, Joe?" Tom asked anxiously as Joe turned north on Michigan Avenue.

"Maybe at some restaurant having breakfast, or, more likely, a bar she's so upset with me. I'm going to work my way over to Clark Street and I'll send you in a few places to see if you can spot her."

Tom was in and out of dozens of bars and restaurants, waving to well-wishers along the way. At several spots Joe double parked and ran into establishments that he and Patty had frequented. Without thinking, Tom jumped in behind the wheel, having of course never driven a motor vehicle, but surprisingly drove on without running over anyone.

As they pulled up to a stop light in front of Wrigley Field, Joe had an idea. "Turn right here."

"On to Addison?" Tom asked, grateful he hadn't yet destroyed Joe's automobile, a beat up 1960 Chevy.

"No. drive along the side of the ballpark. We're going to that fire station."

Joe directed Tom to park on the side of the station so as not to block the pathway engines would be using for an emergency call. A young fireman in a navy short-sleeved shirt with pronounced muscles in his arms stepped out to meet Joe. He recognized Tom immediately and he lit up with a broad smile.

"How you doing?"

"Good," Tom replied shaking his hand.

Joe was a step behind Tom and asked, "Is Patty Dwyer here

by chance? Her old man used to work here."

"You friends?" the fireman asked cautiously and Joe nodded.

"Come on back. Your car will be good there for a while."

Patty was sitting atop a bright red hook and ladder in the tillerman's cab with a can of Schlitz in her hand. For the cool morning she was wearing a Chicago Bears sweatshirt. Her hair was straight and unwashed with the 'peace' symbol on the headband off center.

"Get out of here, Joe," she yelled causing firemen playing cards in the back to turn toward them.

"Patty, it's important that I talk with you," Tom said. "It's very important."

"I'll talk with you, but not him," she said pointing the beer can at Joe.

"I'll be out front," Joe offered. "Take it easy on the beer. The sun's barely up."

"I'll drink what I want," Patty yelled. "You don't seem to care much about me anyhow going off and joining the Marines."

Tom thought she was going to throw the can at Joe and quickly stepped up on the fire engine. He sat on the end of the latter facing Patty waiting for her to calm down a bit. After nearly a minute he spoke in an even tone, "I know you are both mad at, and afraid for Joe. I can see you love him very much." Patty said nothing and turned her face away from Tom. He could see tears forming at the bottom of her eyes. He continued, "I can't say how or why I know this, but he will be fine. I do know that."

After several moments she took a drink from the can of

Schlitz and turned her head back to Tom. "What are you-some kind of soothsayer now? You can tell me what the future will bring?"

"No, not really," Tom lied. "I just know he will be fine. But that's not why I came here today."

"Why then?" She wiped away tears with the sleeve of her sweater.

"There's a problem and I don't want you to get hurt."

"Hurt? What are you talking about?"

Looking around to ensure no one was close by, Tom moved closer to Patty to talk softly. "Those gangsters at Mayor's Row have a lot of money riding against the Cubs and have threatened to harm you and Joe if I keep on playing the way I have."

Patty's blue eyes widened. "Are you serious?"

Tom nodded. "I wish I wasn't, but I am."

Her anger returned. "Those no good...."

"That's how I thought you would react. You're no match for them and I don't want you anywhere they can get to you. I feel responsible for this."

She was silent in thought looking down at the steel floor of the cab, and then abruptly she snapped up. "You're not going to throw any games, are you?"

"Shhh," Tom whispered glancing around with his index finger to his lips. "No. Of course not," he whispered. "It's crucial that the Cubs get into the series. I'm doing it for a friend that's close to me."

"Does Joe know about this?"

Tom shook his head. "He's leaving for California in the morning for basic training, and he might go AWOL if he knew about this. Please go with him. Until the season's over at least. They won't know where you are."

"What about you?" she asked with obvious concern.

"I'll take care of myself. Don't worry about me. Maybe I can see you out in California when we play the Dodgers in a few days."

"But I will be worried." Then she continued with a forced laugh, "Besides, you have the same last name as Joe. How can I not be worried? I'm already scared to death about Joe going to Viet Nam."

"Really, don't worry!"

"You keep saying that," Patty said.

"I realize that, Patty. But please believe me." And then he added, "I've got to get ready. Promise?"

Patty reluctantly agreed that she would go with Joe to California and watch out for him. Tom left them in the hands of the fire department for the time being and walked across Waveland to the ballpark, signing autographs all the way to the clubhouse door.

CHAPTER 10

Wrigley Field was filled to the brim with every seat taken with another two or three thousand standing. The cool of the morning had turned to a mild afternoon with a gentle breeze from the west that brought the aroma of burning leaves over the ballpark. The Cardinals were a formidable team, but it was the Mets that the Cubs must catch up to in order to be in the Series. To do so the Cubs must win their games and the Mets must falter, which they hadn't been doing.

In the back of his mind Tom was troubled by the threats of Johnny Rome, but now that Joe and Patty would be out of the gangster's reach, he had no intention of complying with his demands. He looked forward to the game and couldn't wait to get on the field. But then trouble entered the picture.

The metal passage above the concourse leading from the clubhouse to the dugout had been tampered with and the safety brace at the section needed only to be pulled loose for the entire passage to collapse. Tom was so anxious to get out to the field for batting practice he didn't notice the thug that had been with Johnny Rome at the Ivanhoe was underneath the structure with his beefy hand on the brace. Tom was just a few feet away moving fast when the mobster removed the safety brace. Without warning the structure gave way and Tom fell with the crashing steel that hit the concrete concourse below with a resounding bang. Spectators just seconds below cheering their hero were horrorstruck as he dropped ten feet amidst steel metal bars and lay unconscious as the brute casually walked away.

Teammates following Tom jumped down quickly to assist their star player. It was husky Ron Santo who threw Tom over his shoulder and ran him to the downstairs clubhouse door through a path instantly made by the crowd that was shocked at what had just occurred. Inside the clubhouse the team captain placed an unconscious Tom Hartnett atop a cushioned massage table and called for the team doctor.

In seconds Doctor Kearny appeared, checked Tom's breathing and then carefully felt his body from head to toe. Comfortable that nothing major had been damaged, he then worked on restoring consciousness to the Cub star as teammates formed a circle a prudent distance from the table to give the doctor room to work. Wearing a white shirt and Cub blue tie, the doctor studied Tom's eyes with a light, raising one lid then the other. Having completed his examination a few minutes later with Tom beginning to regain consciousness, Doctor Kearny snapped his medical bag shut and said to Leo, who had moved to the front of the team players, "We'll need to get him to the hospital for tests. He may have a concussion. I'll have an ambulance ready outside."

The clubhouse was silent and morose since the doctor had called for an ambulance. Santo and Hundley and Ferguson Jenkins stood guard over their superstar as the doctor skillfully treated the cuts and bruises visible through Hartnett's tattered uniform that had been torn by the fall. The entire team then moved as the stretcher was wheeled by emergency technicians to the clubhouse door.

Outside a massive crowd had grown with the appearance of an ambulance in fearful anticipation of what was to come. The throng was eerily quiet as number ninety-nine was spotted on the stretcher and then guided expertly into the long vehicle with its engine running and red lights flashing.

Back in the clubhouse chatter had replaced the noiseless tension as those players on the passageway began to relate what had happened. The clamor increased until Santo got up on a chair, not paying attention to any damage his cleats might do to it, and yelled out once the room had quieted down, "Listen up! I don't know how this accident happened but we've got some big shoes to fill. Hartnett's gotten us back on the track we should have been on." A roar of concurrence came from the players, and then Santo continued, "We can't let Tom down. We need to win!"

More like a team taking a pep talk in a football locker room, the Cubs cheered rowdily and charged out the door that would take them onto the concourse where they intermingled with the fans who cheered them on as they followed them into the stands and down to the dugout.

The Cardinals didn't have a chance. The rejuvenated and determined Cubs displayed a Herculean effort, pounding the ball out of the park and making incredible plays in the field. Six bases were stolen with even Ferguson Jenkins, the great pitcher, doubling and then stealing third base. The Cubs won by ten runs and in the stands Johnny Rome fretted that his sure bet might turn sour. But he still felt that the Cubs by themselves were losers, and that Tom Hartnett would be the essential piece of the puzzle for the Cubs to win. He must make sure that Hartnett would not be able to play.

CHAPTER 11

Tom had fully regained consciousness by the time a few of his teammates entered the hospital room to look in on him. Groggy, he was still undergoing tests when Fergie Jenkins handed him the ball he hit off the vines for a double that was signed by the entire team, including Leo Durocher.

"They say you'll be out of here by morning," Santo said in an earnest voice.

"Fine with me," Tom stated with eyelids drooping. "I'm ready."

"Not so fast," a young doctor said swiftly cutting through the players to Tom's bed. He glanced over several charts attached to a clip board at the foot of his bed, and then checked Tom's eyes and did a onceover on his vitals. He raised two fingers a good two feet from Tom's face and asked, "How many fingers do you see?"

"At least a half dozen," Tom answered, causing a few of the players to chuckle.

The doctor nodded and wrote a few words on the chart, and then looked up at his patient. "Okay if I talk in front of this gang?"

"Sure. They'd probably otherwise cause a ruckus you don't need here."

"We still have to do more tests, but I'm quite sure you have a concussion."

"What does that mean, doc?"

"That means you likely won't be playing baseball for at least a few days. I imagine it's generally hard enough hitting a major league pitcher throwing one ball, let alone a half dozen."

"I'm not sure if you've seen Tom hit," Billy Williams joked. "He may just be able to hit those half dozen pitches at the same time." Collective laughter came from the players as a middle-aged sturdy nurse with strong arms pushed through to take care of her routine tasks.

"Out of the way!" she scolded the players and the doctor smiled and said, "You'd better take heed. She could be a Mets fan."

"I'm a Cubs fan, mind you," she snapped. "But this isn't Wrigley Field for Pete's sake. And I don't want to see any tobacco chewed in here."

"Maybe if Tom gives her an autograph, she'll ease up a bit," Hundley said in his southern drawl.

"I'll get any autographs I want once all of you get out of here."

Wishing to stay with their fallen star, the Cubs protested but to no avail as the nurse was adamant in clearing the room.

Santo was the last to leave repeating the team's commitment to Tom and the need for the man who had only been with them a short time but had made an incredible difference in the Cubs' performance. "We'll take care of business here, Tom, but we could sure use you for the Dodger series out in L.A."

Drowsy from pain medicine, Tom smiled and then fell off to sleep as the Cub captain tapped Tom's hand with his.

CHAPTER 12

Santo was true to his word as the Cubs swept the Cardinal series and found themselves a game and a half behind the amazing Mets with the Dodger series in Los Angeles next, to determine if the Mets or Cubs would win the National League East to play Atlanta for the trip to the Series. The atmosphere in Chicago was ecstatic with returned confidence that this would be the year.

When the news that Tom had been released from the hospital after his tragic fall and cleared to play, Chicagoans were beside themselves. Work was at a near standstill as the Cubs were the topic around office water coolers. The Braves would be a piece of cake. It was the Mets that were the key to getting into the Series. The Cubs had to win both games out west, and the Mets needed to lose their two games against the Cincinnati Reds.

A cold front with steady drizzle from a grey sky had moved over Chicago, making the trip out to sunny California even that much more welcome. The chartered United flight was uncharacteristically quiet with players concentrating on the decisive games ahead instead of their normal frolicking and flirting with the stewardesses. Moving sideways down the aisle with a bag hanging from his shoulder, Bill Daley took a seat next to Tom.

"How's the head, kid?" he asked.

"Better, Bill. I can only see one of you now."

The reporter chuckled, "Lucky you." For a few moments he

was silent in thought and then said, "I'm going to look for Ted Williams while we're in Los Angeles. After I've seen my daughter, of course."

"Where will you look?" Tom asked and then added with the limited knowledge of the short time he has been in Los Angeles, "That's a lot of city out there."

"A good question, Tom. A good question." The reporter hesitated as if he was working on a decision. He scratched his jaw and said, "I never thought I would believe in such things, but for some reason I think it was intended that I met and drove Ted Williams to the Ambassador Hotel since now I have come to know you. You know by the way that we're staying at the Ambassador."

Tom smiled with a look to imply the absurdity of what Daley had just said, but wondering about the coincidence of the team staying at this hotel.

"I know it sounds outlandish, but so many things don't add up," the reporter added. "It's like I'm in a dream world."

Tom continued to smile and then slid down in his seat and hunched his powerful shoulders to get more comfortable. "Speaking of dream worlds, I think that's where I'm going now." Still a bit worn out by the fall, he closed his eyes and slept the rest of the way to Los Angeles.

CHAPTER 13

At the Los Angeles airport Tom shed his jacket stepping down the metal staircase that had been rolled out to the plane and saw Joe and Patty waving at him from behind the waist high chain-link fence behind which friends and family waited to greet passengers.

Over the fence Tom shook hands with Joe and hugged Patty. "What are you doing here?" Tom said anxiously looking around for any sign of Johnny Rome.

"I told him this morning about the threats," Patty admitted. "With you coming out here, I didn't think there would be the danger of Joe going back to Chicago."

"I'm worried about Rome coming out here. He's probably getting desperate since we swept the Cardinals and are only a game and a half behind New York."

The normally lighthearted Joe had a dark look about him and said, "Mob or not, that jerk's not going to threaten Patty!"

Patty smiled and took Joe's hand in hers. "He doesn't want them hurting his wife!"

Tom leaned back with surprise and gave a puzzled look to each. Patty laughed. "We drove over to Las Vegas yesterday and got hitched. We've got a room here at the Disneyland Hotel." She moved closer to Joe and leaned up to kiss him on the cheek. To Tom she said, "I'm taking you at your word that he'll come back all right from Viet Nam. But no kids! I'm not going to bring up a child just to get killed off in some war!"

Joe winked at Tom. "I'm working on that."

"Fat chance," Patty scorned with tightened lips as she fingered her headband with the red peace symbol. Tom was afraid she might slug him there on the tarmac as a plane taxiing by made it hard to hear, so he indicated with his hand that they go inside.

Inside, they took row chairs by the gate with Joe and Tom sitting sideways to face one another and Patty grabbed a seat in the middle.

"We read about your fall," Tom said. "Are you all right?"

"I'm fine," Tom replied. Taking a quick scan of his surroundings, he added in a discreet voice, "We found that a brace had been tampered with. My guess is Johnny Rome was involved, and I would presume he's out here with so much to lose."

"That no good..." Joe started, but was stopped by Tom.

"That's why I didn't want Patty to say anything to you in Chicago. That's his turf. You can't take them on there. For that matter you can't take them on anywhere. They're the mob!"

"Listen," Joe retorted. "Nobody threatens my wife! He can be Al Capone for all I care."

At that moment Bill Daley came by after stopping in the men's room. "Better step it up, Tom. The bus to the Ambassador will be leaving soon."

"Meet a couple of friends of mine from Chicago, Bill," Tom offered. "Joe and Patty Hartnett."

The reporter took off his straw hat and shook their hands. "Bill Daley with the *Trib*. Hartnett? You related to Tom?"

"No. Just a coincidence," Joe replied still agitated by the gangster's threats.

Daley nodded staring at the pair for several moments. He

seemed to be curious about anyone or anything linked to the baseball phenomenon. Then he turned to Tom and said, "I'll see you on the bus."

Once the reporter was out of earshot, Tom said, "Please stay out of sight. These guys are serious. I don't want either of you to get hurt." A frightening thought came to Tom for the first time, wondering if the future could be changed if something happened to either of his grandparents. It was a cold chill that made him weak.

"Are you okay?" Patty asked seeing that Tom had turned pale.

"Sure," Tom replied shaking off his apprehension. "Call me at the Ambassador when you get checked in at Disneyland. And keep an eye out for Johnny Rome." Tom turned and waved as he broke into a jog to catch up with the team.

Joe and Patty looked at each other and smiled and Joe winked with an understanding that they would take care of each other. They would watch for Johnny Rome, but all they really had to do was to look around a nearby ticket kiosk where the gangster's muscle was covertly watching them.

CHAPTER 14

Two hours later the pair of Chicago mobsters used a house key lifted from a maid to enter Joe and Patty's room in Disneyland while Joe was taking a shower. Patty was surveying the magnificent sites of the spectacular park from a balcony when Rome's muscular goon slipped up behind her and stifled any screams from Patty with a chloroform soaked cloth that put her asleep almost immediately. He quickly and quietly whisked her from the room and dumped her in a waiting laundry hamper to roll her from the hotel to a waiting car.

Drying off a few minutes later in the bathroom Joe called out to Patty, "Let's go down for a drink." He was puzzled that she didn't answer, but figured she might have headed to the hotel lobby ahead of him. Then Joe saw both room keys on the table and a chair turned over on the balcony. An uneasy feeling came over him as he feared immediately what had happened. He picked up the phone and asked the hotel operator to connect him with the Ambassador Hotel. Several seconds later he was connected to Tom's room. "This is Joe," he shouted when Tom answered. "They've got Patty."

"What happened?" Tom retorted, dreading that this would occur. He wished he had never dreamed that he could have made Gramps happy putting the Cubs in the World Series. Gramps was miserable. Tom had only heard Gramps talk of Patty so he had never seen her. Could something bad have happened to her at this time due Tom trying to change history? Or did something happen that Gramps never talked about?

Frantic, Joe hastily described what took place and Tom was silent in thought for several moments. And then he said, "They won't hurt her unless I don't do what they say. I'm sure they'll contact me soon."

"What will you do?"

"I need to think this through."

"I've got to find her. I love her, Tom!"

"I know, Joe. We'll get her back. Don't worry. Give me your phone number at Disneyland. I'll let you know when I hear something." Tom hung up after getting the number and was surprised at his capacity to think the matter through knowing that he couldn't jeopardize his future grandmother and at the same time fix the game of baseball. He didn't need to wait long to hear about Patty as Johnny Rome called twenty minutes later. "Hey hero boy, I've got the girl and you know what I'll do if you don't do the right thing."

"Put her on the phone so I know she's all right."

A few seconds later Patty audaciously cried on the other end, "Don't let these bums talk you into anything!" She was about to add something when she was pulled away from the phone and Tom could hear her yelling and cursing the gangsters. A loud slap followed and Patty cursed them again. Johnny Rome returned on the line. "If she keeps it up, I'll take care of her just for kicks."

"Don't do anything," Tom said. "I'll do what you want. How do I get her back?"

"After the second game, when I know my money's good, I'll get word to you where to find her."

"How can I trust you? I'll need something better than that."

"Can't do, slugger. I have all the cards. You've got to go with this. And you'd better tell her to shut her trap if she knows what's good for her."

"Put her back on the line."

"You'd better not buckle under these bozos!" she shouted so loud it hurt Tom's ears.

"Patty. Listen and listen carefully. Joe and I will figure something out. In the meantime, we just need you to stay alive. Can you do that?"

"Of course I can. You think I'm some kind of idiot like these two dolts."

Tom groaned and heard another slap over the phone.

The gangster came back on the line. "Let's see how smart you are, slugger. And don't even think about calling the police if you ever want to see her alive again." The line went dead.

CHAPTER 15

From the start Tom had never thought of getting the authorities involved. How would he explain himself if questioned to any extent? No, he must deal with this sleazy and dangerous character on his own. But how? He was not part of that world. He had no weapons to speak of, and probably wouldn't know what to do if he did. But he couldn't return to his true life years later leaving Joe and Patty at the mercy of these gangsters. Or would he be able to return to 2015, he wondered with a sudden sense of panic? How would he return? But as soon as this apprehension came to him, he forced it out. There was plenty of time to worry about that. For now, his grandmother's life was at stake.

Helpless to really do anything, Tom slept little that night, as did Joe in his room at Disneyland after Tom had called to relay the conversation with Johnny Rome. The next morning Joe met Tom in the lobby of the Ambassador as the team was getting ready to leave for Dodger Stadium.

"Did you hear anything more?" Joe asked. Tom shook his head.

"There's got to be something we can do," Joe said. He was nervous and not his jovial self.

"We will, Joe," Tom assured, patting a strong hand on Joe's shoulder. "We will."

At that moment Leo approached the two and asked Tom, "I need a few seconds in private with you, Tom."

"Sure." He looked at Joe who was in thought and not paying

attention to the Cub manager. "Leo, meet my Gr.....; my friend Joe Hartnett."

"Mr. Durocher," Joe acknowledged shaking hands.

"Hartnett. You guys related?"

"Just a coincidence," Tom replied answering for Joe.

"How about that," he said to Joe, taking Tom's elbow to guide him to privacy, "We won't be a minute."

Once out of earshot of anyone, Leo said, "They've got Drysdale going today and Osteen tomorrow. Drysdale's having a bad year and Osteen's hot. I talked with Doc and he said it would be a good idea to give you one more day's rest. We'll beat Drysdale, but I'll need you against Osteen. So you'll be sitting out today."

Trying not to show his relief, Tom nodded. "Sure coach. Whatever you say."

"I told you to call me Leo, kid. You're making me feel old."

Tom smiled and sheepishly nodded again.

The legendary Cub manager was correct in his thinking. With Tom on the bench the Cubs still beat Drysdale and the Dodgers easily, twelve to four. Santo, Banks, Hundley and Williams all homered-Banks twice and, as important, the Mets lost their game to the Pirates. Still up by a half a game, the next day would tell the tale. If the Mets won, they would play Atlanta in the playoffs. If they lost and the Cubs won, the Cubs would play Atlanta. If the Cubs lost they would be through for the year regardless of the Mets outcome. With the Mets playing an evening game in New York, the Cubs, assuming they would win, would then have to wait for the outcome of the later game back east to learn their destiny.

CHAPTER 16

The afternoon was perfect for baseball with the temperature in the upper 70's under a clear soft blue cloudless sky. Even though the Dodgers had been long out of contention, Dodger Stadium was without an empty seat and the aisles found fans standing above the last rows. It was a Cub crowd. Many that had traveled from Chicago and countless were former Chicagoans now residing in southern California. Electricity flowed throughout the ballpark with a constant buzz hanging in the air.

Tom was in the Cub dugout contemplating his dilemma. With Joe in his room the night before, Tom heard from Johnny Rome and let Joe listen in. Greatly disappointed that the Cubs had won even without Tom, the gangster was still confident that the Cubs were losers and would get beat out by the Mets, as long as Tom cooperated. When Tom asked to again hear Patty's voice, she got on the phone with the same energy level as the night before, cussing out her captors, which, of course, was followed by a couple of slapping sounds. Gritting his teeth, Joe's eyes had narrowed after Tom hung up the phone. If Rome had been within arm's reach, Joe would likely have had to be on the run the rest of his life for doing in one of the mob's own.

"Any ideas yet?" Joe asked Tom, sitting alongside of him in the dugout. Leo had approved Tom's request for Joe to sit in the dugout.

Tom shook his head. "So far, no. But I will."

Osteen was at the top of his game. The slight compact left

hander was an artist on the mound, throwing a fastball that sunk at the last second along with a wicked sinker that batters mostly pounded into the ground. Leo was right that the Cubs needed Tom for this game, but he too, was having uncharacteristic trouble with the masterful Osteen. He did hit two towering foul balls that would have easily been home runs if they had remained fair. As it was, Tom had not yet picked up a hit with one out already in the ninth inning with the Dodgers ahead two to nothing. The rest of the Cubs had fared about the same, as Osteen had held the visitors from Wrigley to three scattered singles. The Cub fans' hopes for a chance at the Series began to wane with a general feeling that the great Tom Hartnett hadn't yet healed enough to save the day, and Osteen was too good to beat today.

There was a chance, though, as the Cubs had the meat of their order still to bat; Santo, Williams, Banks and then Tom. In the dugout Tom was next to Joe at the far end. Their minds were both on the game and on the whereabouts of Patty. "Where do you think they have her?" Joe said nervously bouncing one of his legs and running his hand over a hairless scalp that had been shaved for boot camp.

"I think I saw them sitting behind us a couple of rows up," Tom related in a hushed tone.

"Patty's probably gagged in the trunk of their car then," Joe said. "They wouldn't leave her at a hotel. If so, there's just so much air in a car trunk." Neither one spoke of what they were thinking – that Patty might not be alive. They had to assume that she was.

Santo brought their attention back to the game when he hit a shot that nearly tore Osteen's ear off. He thought of stretching the hit into a double but wisely held at first base. Williams then hit a sharp grounder to the first baseman who juggled the ball and was only able to force Santo at second. Banks was up with two out and a man on first, and Tom selected his bat to get some practice swings in the on-deck circle. It was there that he glanced back in the stands above the Cub dugout. Johnny Rome was smiling with his muscle in the chair to his left. Tom had an urge to take the leaded practice bat and smash it across the mobster's rotten face. It was then that he began to formulate a plan, but Banks needed to get on base for it to even be a possibility.

The Cub great, nearing the end of his career, was still a dangerous hitter and Osteen took his time to carefully pitch to the future Hall of Famer. He wouldn't give Banks anything good that he could land in the left field stands. Banks worked Osteen to a full count and went after a low slider on the outside corner, looping it over the second baseman. At first it appeared the second baseman might pull the ball in over his shoulder but it then fell just past him. Banks was on first and Williams on second with Tom coming up.

The crowd became alive and was in a sudden frenzy as Tom finished his practice swings. While he waited for the infielders and coach to visit with Osteen, he saw Rome from the corner of his eye above the Dodgers' first base dugout. The gangster shook his head slowly. The message was clear. Finally, the home plate umpire, a large man with a red face, trotted half way to the mound to break up the meeting, and Osteen then picked up the rosin bag to dry his hand. Amid the roaring crowd Tom stepped up to the plate batting right handed against the left handed Osteen and dug his cleats into the ground for a firm footing. What he had to do was abruptly clear. Until that moment he had been uncertain as to what he could do. The first pitch was a low dropping fastball out of the strike zone, but Tom didn't take the bait. The next pitch he figured would need to be a strike but likely on the outside corner. If so, that was the one he wanted, and it was. The ball started out of the strike zone coming fast and then at the last second snapped over the outside corner. Tom delayed his swing just enough with a smooth powerful swing to foul the ball off to the right. The ball rocketed at twice the speed of the pitch straight at Johnny Rome and his thug friend. It hit the muscle first square on the temple and then caught Rome between the eyes. A hush came over the crowd as both were jetted backward over their chairs and lay unconscious as a space was made by those sitting nearby. Fortuitously, no other fan was hit by the savage smash.

The crucial game was delayed for several minutes while emergency personnel tended to the pair, carting both out on stretchers. And then with attention back on the field, the home plate umpire positioned himself behind the catcher and yelled out in a strong voice, "Play Ball!"

Osteen stretched his back and shoulders looking at Tom, bat on shoulder and ready sixty feet and six inches away in the batter's box. He had a one ball and one strike count on him. Not sure what had happened in the stands behind him, Joe was standing and leaning forward in the dugout, his mind still on Patty's whereabouts. He watched Tom at bat and saw a natural if there ever were one, readying himself at the plate. Tom seemed taller than he was with the bat and the man appearing as one.

As Osteen wound up, there was no doubt in Joe's mind as to

what would happen. The pitch was fast and high, Osteen tried to get one past Tom. It was certainly a mistake by the otherwise crafty pitcher as Tom crushed the ball. Barely before necks could turn, it cleared the wall and then the stadium, crashing through the windshield of a car parked in the lot behind left field. Pandemonium prevailed as the Cubs went ahead by a run, plenty for the Cubs, as Durocher brought in Kenny Holtzman to pitch. The great lefty faced three batters and took care of all three in short order. The Cubs had won and now just needed the Mets to lose. And the initial reports were good as the east coast night game had just begun. The Pirates had already scored six runs in the first.

The clubhouse was ecstatic. Champaign was sprayed in all directions and on everyone. But Tom and Joe weren't celebrating. A few days ago Joe would have given anything to be in the Cubs' locker room after such a victory, but now his main concern was for Patty. Once Tom had explained what had happened to Johnny Rome and his pal, they both agreed with their earlier conclusion. Patty must be tied up and gagged in the trunk of their car, but how would they find her in time so she didn't suffocate? They wouldn't allow themselves to think that she's not alive.

"Congratulations, Tom," Bill Daley said in an unusually tired voice.

"Is there anything wrong, Bill," Tom said taking his mind momentarily off of Patty's predicament.

The reporter smiled. "Remember that guy I was talking to you about – Ted Williams?"

"Sure."

"Something happened last night back at the Ambassador I

want to talk with you about."

"Can we talk later? I've got something urgent to do with Joe here."

"No problem. Maybe on the flight back to Chicago." And then he added, "By the way, it turns out you accomplished something a lot of Syndicate boys have been trying to do. Those two guys that got carried out from your foul ball are with the mob. Johnny Rome and a guy named Frank Carbone. Carbone didn't make it and Rome's memory is probably shot."

"Mobster's. No kidding?"

"If anyone was to be hit, you picked the right ones. That's for sure. They're as bad as they come."

"We've got to go," Joe pressed, nudging Tom's arm.

"I'll see you on the plane," Tom said to the reporter as he slipped into his street clothes without even showering.

Outside the ballpark Tom noticed that many cars had left and there were few fans waiting, in contrast to Wrigley Field after a game. He mentioned this to Joe who replied, "That's Dodger fans for you. They don't hang around."

They both looked over the parking lot in thought wondering how they would strategize a search since there were still a number of cars left and several lots to choose from. With his hands on his hips Tom glanced around and said, "They were sitting in the first base box seats, so they likely parked in this lot that's closest to their gate. But what will we look for?"

"Look for a rental car. They must have come in one."

"How will I know it's a rental?" Tom replied.

"On the back bumper will be a sticker for Hertz, Avis or one of the other companies. I know that from working at the airport." He pointed to the right. "You check the cars in that direction and I'll do the others. Patty's resourceful. Look for some sign she might have left."

They started out, both realizing there couldn't be much time left, if any. Neither could accept that Patty might have already suffocated. They searched hastily but methodically, aware that they couldn't miss any signs. Each came across a number of rental cars and they would pound on the trunks, but to no avail. Several minutes later each had reached the end of the parking lot and signaled to one another that neither had had any luck so far. In addition to coming up empty the sun was beginning to set and it would soon be dark. Tom was beginning to panic. Without breaking windows to open trunks on every rental car, there was no place to turn. And then it dawned on him that Rome and his pal might have hotwired a car to leave Patty in the trunk to suffocate, and then take a taxi back to the airport. It was a long shot and he had to work fast. He called out to Joe what he planned to do and Joe signaled that he understood.

Tom raced back and forth checking cars without rental stickers that he had passed on earlier. But he was having no success with this either and was becoming quite discouraged and then he saw it. Stuck in the narrow trunk seam of a black Pontiac was a white head band with a peace symbol – Patty's head band. He screamed for Joe who sprinted across the lot to see what Tom had found. Without hesitation, Joe smashed in the driver's window with his forearm and reached his bleeding arm in to pop the trunk. And there she was, gagged and very much alive, kicking savagely at anything close to her. Both Tom and Joe stood back to avoid being struck. Joe actually laughed which infuriated Patty even more as she rolled out of the trunk and fell comically to the parking lot pavement with her hands tied behind her back. Tom rushed to her to remove the gag and help her up. Once on her feet still with the hands bound, she moved to Joe and kicked him hard on a shin. "What took you so long?" she shouted over sobs. "You know I'm afraid of the dark!"

"Let me at least kiss you," Joe snorted. He took her in his arms and she responded to his request, kissing him long and hard as Tom freed her hands from behind. But then she pushed away and slugged Joe in the chest and yelled, "It was so dark in there, I thought I was going to have a heart attack." And then she snapped, "Where are those jerks by the way, and why is your arm bleeding, Joe?"

"Let's get out of here," Tom urged. "We've got a broken window here I'd rather not have to explain."

"We still have a room at Disneyland," Joe said. "Let's get a cab." To Tom he asked, "When do you fly back?"

"The plane leaves at midnight, so we've got plenty of time. I could use a shower anyhow if you don't mind."

"I'll go first," Patty demanded. "Those no good buffoons wouldn't let me even wash my face for three days."

Forty-five minutes later they were in the room at the Disneyland Hotel, and had just heard the good news on television that the Pirates were up nine runs going into the ninth. They couldn't lose!

CHAPTER 17

At quarter to six Pacific Time the bad news was broadcasted to Cub fans throughout the world. The Mets had staged an unbelievable comeback scoring ten runs in the ninth inning to beat the Pirates and win the division crown to play Atlanta for a slot in the World Series.

"Oh my gosh," Patty cried dripping wet wrapped in a Disneyland robe on hearing the announcement on television. "What happened? They were up by nine runs going into the ninth!"

Sitting on a chair slumped over with hands folded between spread legs, Joe shook his head smiling with astonishment. "The Cubs," was all he said shaking his head looking down at the floor.

"I'm going down to the lobby to get some gum," Tom said, dejected, wondering why he was here if the Cubs weren't going to the series. Joe acknowledged Tom with a wave still with his head drooping and Patty just mumbled to herself.

Realizing that this was the hotel that he was staying at with Gramps before this bizarre journey had begun, Tom walked into a lobby strikingly different than the luxurious hotel lobby he and Gramps had come to. A rug was worn and furniture was plain. It was an ordinary motor inn, but what it did have was a monorail that stopped above the hotel entrance to transport guests to the Disneyland park, located a few hundred yards away. Tom bought a couple of Mouseketeer hats in the gift shop for Joe and Patty and decided to take the monorail into the park to see the sights.

Tom stayed on the monorail for some time, enjoying the wonderful park from above, and then decided appropriately to get off at Fantasyland with the hats under his arm in a bag. The 'Alice In Wonderland' ride was especially intriguing to Tom for some reason, and he asked the attendant, a college-age young man, where he needed to pay for the ride.

"You need a Park ticket," the attendant replied and then added offhandedly, "It's slow right now. Go ahead and get in one of the cars."

"Thanks," Tom replied. "I've only got a little time before I leave, anyhow."

He stepped into a car and set the package containing the hats on the seat next to him. The ride took off and Tom marveled as might a small child at the Wonderland sights. As a lark he took one of the hats from the bag and set it on his head, fingering one of the black ears. It was around the third turn that Tom began to feel odd. He sensed a spell of vertigo and then a buzzing sound came into his ears. The light of day disappeared and it was as if he had suddenly lost his sight. He was falling in a vortex, spinning out of control. Colors began to appear, at first imageless, but then taking shape. In a few seconds Gramps came into view, forty-six years older than the man he had left just a few minutes prior, sitting down at a table ahead of him in the Orleans Café.

CHAPTER 18

"There'll be one more in a few minutes," Joe Hartnett said to the waiter, a thin middle-aged man with a narrow mustache, as Tommy took a wrought-iron chair across from Gramps. "But I know Tommy will want the 'Mickey's Cheesy Macaroni'," he added, winking at his grandson. "Go ahead and bring one of those now to get started with." Joe pushed back his blue Cubs hat, revealing his short gray hair. Tommy couldn't understand how so much had happened during the short time it took to walk from the front door, the last moment he remembered before his adventure began, to the table in the courtyard. How could that possibly be? He surveyed his hands and arms and saw that they had diminished considerably in size and muscle from just a few seconds ago. He was feeling lightheaded.

"You okay, son," Joe asked with concern, noticing Tommy's drawn face.

"I'm okay, Gramps. Maybe a little hungry."

"Well, that Cheesy Macaroni should take care of that in short order."

Tommy smiled, realizing how much he loved his grandfather and how glad he was that he had gotten to know him as a young man, even if it was for just a short period of time. A couple of minutes later the waiter brought a heaping portion of Cheesy Macaroni and set the plate in front of Tommy whose eyes widened considerably at the dish. Joe grinned and nodded to his grandson to begin eating. It was at that moment that an older woman appeared over the waiter's shoulder and smiled at Joe. Her face was wrinkled with blue eyes and her gray hair was up in a bun. She wore a navy Bears' sweatshirt with orange letters. Busy on surveying his meal, Tommy hadn't noticed her until she spoke.

"So this is Tommy!" the lady said. Tommy looked up and didn't need to be told who she was. He was looking at his grandmother!

The boy did have the presence of mind not to acknowledge that he had already met her, but in a different life. He waited.

"Tommy boy, this is your grandmother," Joe said standing up, moving his chair back. Tommy put down his fork and stood up also.

Patty looked at her grandson for the first time for several moments and then said with her hands on her cheeks, "Oh my gosh, he's just precious!" She bent down and wrapped her arms around Tommy and held him tight for a long period. Tears flowed down her face until she let him go to compose herself, and then wiped her eyes dry with a hankie. She reached her hand out to affectionately touch Joe's.

"Hi," Tommy simply addressed his grandmother with warm eyes.

"You sit down and eat your meal," Patty said and took the chair between the two. While the boy ate, she just watched him with gleaming eyes. And then she turned to Joe. "I've been so foolish and selfish."

"You were scared," Joe said.

She mused for a few moments, and then said, "Yes, you're right, and look what I've missed."

"Are you coming back to Chicago, grandma?" Tommy asked.

"Yes, dear, I am." She eyed Joe. "Your grandfather and I have a lot of catching up to do. And I understand your father is going to be transferred back from overseas."

Tommy turned excitedly to Gramps who nodded with a smile, "That's right, Tommy. Your father will be home in a couple of weeks."

"You'll see him too, right, Grandma?"

"Of course, dear. Like I said, I have an awful lot of catching up to do." She stared at her grandson for several moments with tears again forming in her eyes, and then she grasped his hand. "I'm so sorry about your mother."

Her touch felt wonderful. "I wish I had known her."

Patty replied, "I know, honey. I know."

The waiter came by to see if Joe and Patty were ready to order, and Joe said, "Give us all Mickey's Cheesy Macaroni."

Just as the waiter left, a man that appeared to be a few years older than Joe and Patty was walking by and noticed their Cub and Bear clothing.

"There's some Chicagoans! Mind if I say hello?"

"I know you," Joe said. "You're Bill Daley with the *Tribune* sports."

"Yes," he said offering his hand. "But I've been retired for several years."

Joe stood and shook it. "I enjoyed your column. Meet my wife and our grandson."

Tommy stood and shook his hand as did Patty, but then she chided the former reporter, "You've said a lot of bad things about the Cubs. You made me mad."

Daley laughed. "Not as mad as me. I lived and died with them over an entire career."

Joe noticed that Patty's eyes were narrowing and her teeth were gritting so he squeezed her hand as a signal to behave.

"Have we met?" Daley asked, eyeing Joe curiously.

"I don't think so," Joe replied as Tommy leaned backward a bit as he had recognized the reporter also the second that he spoke.

"Humph," he murmured and looked at Tommy. "There's something familiar about you, too." Tommy said nothing as a boy his age would likely do. And then, shrugging off the thought, Daley continued, "It's just good to see Cub and Bear fans. Living out here now, I don't see many."

"You don't live in Chicago anymore?" Joe asked.

"My daughter stayed out here after going to UCLA and had a family. I wanted to be close to her and my grandchildren." He hesitated, and then added, "There's also a person I got to know out here years ago, in 1968, that I'm trying to get back in touch with."

The distant look on Daley's face kindled Joe's curiosity. "1968. A lot went on back then." He winked at Patty who jabbed her husband in the leg with her knuckles. She knew he was alluding to her political crusading days.

"Yes. A lot did," the retired newsman mused, seeming to be on the verge of a decision, and then, sitting down on the forth chair, asked, "Did you two follow the Cubs in 1969?"

"Did we!" Patty cried. "That team about put us into an asylum!"

Daley nodded somberly. "I have a question. How many games were the Cubs behind the Mets at the end of the season?"

"What, are you trying to torture us?" Patty exclaimed.

"Eight games," Joe chuckled derisively. "Eight full games!"

"See, no one seems to remember what I do; that the Cubs lost on the last day of the season. They beat the Dodgers out here, but the Mets had to lose that night and came back from nine runs down in the ninth to win."

"But how could that be?" Joe asked, puzzled that a reporter wouldn't have that information clear at hand. "No one would forget something like that." He sadly speculated that the former *Tribune* writer might be suffering from dementia.

"I came to that realization years ago," Daley replied. "No one I've ever talked to remembers what I remember. They thought I was going nuts; myself included. But those last five weeks of the season are still as clear as day to me. A ballplayer named Hartnett, Tom Hartnett, came out of nowhere and just dominated the game." Tom and Patty glanced at each other while Tommy worked on his Cheesy Macaroni appearing not to pay attention to the discussion. "His home runs were at least six hundred feet and he could throw a ball on a line six feet off the ground from the outfield wall to home plate."

"I won't say it," Joe said. "You've probably heard it a million times already."

"No, I understand. That's physically impossible. I agree, but I saw it happen." He smiled in thought and then added," I just like to tell the story to Cub fans in hopes that somebody else recalls what I do. I was supposed to talk to Hartnett on the plane home about another strange happening. I'm talking about the occurrence the year before in 1968, but he never showed at the airport." He looked off and said snapping his fingers, "Just disappeared like that!"

"What about 1968?" Patty broke in. "I'm always curious about those days."

Joe winked at Tommy and Patty, seeing Joe from the corner of her eye, jabbed him in the ribs.

Daley commenced to gladly tell the story of Ted Williams, clarifying to Joe that he wasn't the great Red Sox slugger, and their unfortunate late arrival at the Ambassador Hotel. Then he described the futile effort to locate the mysterious Williams after that fateful June night. Every chance Daley got he took time off to travel to Los Angeles under the guise to his employer of visiting his daughter in search of Williams.

"I was about to give it up when the Cubs stayed at the Ambassador for the Dodger series in 1969. It was the night of the first game back at the hotel. I decided to go see the kitchen where Kennedy's killer was standing before he shot him, and who was there working as a busboy, but Ted Williams."

"Why was he there?" asked Patty who seemed to be intrigued by the story.

"He said he couldn't go back."

"What did that mean?" she said.

"He couldn't go back to wherever he came from," Daley explained. "It was never clear to me, but I think he was sent, perhaps from the future, somehow to prevent the killing of Bobby Kennedy and he didn't make it in time. And then he disappeared again." Tommy squirmed in his chair with a sense of anxiety, wondering if something as such might be in store for him.

"But that's fantasy," Joe said. "Something out of science fiction."

"Of course it is. I never believed in these things before, but how can I not with all that's happened? I come to Disneyland because Ted mentioned that night at the Ambassador that somehow the Park was connected to all of this. I lost him after the night in 1969 and have been trying to find him ever since."

"You've been coming here for over forty-five years?" Patty asked with astonishment.

Daley nodded. "Yes. I'm here so much they've given me a lifetime pass." And then he added with a chuckle, "It doesn't hurt that I write up articles in the *Trib* on Disneyland from time to time. I have a guest column still with the paper."

"But why is it so important that you find Ted Williams?" Patty inquired.

"That's a good question. There's got to be a reason I was brought into this, first with Ted and then a year later with Hartnett. Thousands of people witnessed the same things I did with Hartnett, but no one seems to remember but me. There's no record of Hartnett playing or even of the games the last five weeks of the season. The two Dodger games out here didn't even exist according to Major League Baseball. Officially, the Cubs ended up that horrible season with the Mets in Chicago, eight games out, as you say. What does all that mean?"

Joe shrugged and shook his head. "I don't know what to say, Bill. It is no doubt very strange."

Daley smiled and pushed his chair back standing up. "Thanks for listening to me. It's good to get this off my chest every so often and it's always good to talk with the fans." He shook hands with all three and left.

Still standing while the retired reporter turned a corner to another part of the restaurant, they were silent for several moments. And then Patty said to Joe, "Any reason you didn't mention that our names are Hartnett?"

"He's confused enough. I didn't want to add to his worries."

She leaned toward Joe and stretched up to kiss him on the cheek. "You're sweet, you know that? After we finish eating we'll all take a ride on the Tunnel of Love."

"Aren't you afraid of the dark, Grandma?" Tommy broke in.

Patty look at Tommy strangely and said, "Who told you that, darling? I was at one time but grew out of it."

Tommy's face reddened, realizing his mistake, when Gramps said, "I probably did some time ago. I talk about you a lot." Patty kissed Joe on the lips a long time and said, "I've missed you so much, honey."

The waiter arrived with their meals and they sat back down. Tommy now knew the purpose for his journey. It was not for a Cub World Series. They would have to accomplish that on their own in time. He was meant to know his wonderful grandmother and help bring her and Gramps back together. With relish, the young boy returned to his Mickey's Cheesy Macaroni as Gramps and Tommy's newly found grandmother affectionately touched each other's hand.

THE END

www.ingramcontent.com/pod-product-compliance
Lightning Source LLC
Chambersburg PA
CBHW020533120726
47904CB00003B/1062